PENELOPE CRUMB ... A *THIEF?!*

"I've got to go see Felix. He had some people in his apartment to paint, and he thinks they took some things."

My cheeks start to burn. "Took some things?"

Mom grabs her keys from the hall table and then shakes her head. "I don't know how he can tell anything's missing, with the way he keeps that place."

"Something's missing? What's he missing?"

Then I cup my hands over my ears because I'm afraid what she's going to say. But somehow her voice still gets through my fingers because I can still hear Mom say, "Probably nothing. You know Felix." And just when I think it's safe to take my hands away from my ears, she says, "I'm not sure—something about a camera."

That's when I practically go dead.

OTHER BOOKS YOU MAY ENJOY

PENELOPE CRUMB

CRUMB NEVER FORGETS

SHAWN K. STOUT

with art by VALERIA DOCAMPO

PUFFIN BOOKS
An Imprint of Penguin Group (USA) Inc.

PUFFIN BOOKS
An imprint of Penguin Young Readers Group
Published by the Penguin Group
Penguin Group (USA) Inc.
375 Hudson Street
New York, New York 10014, U.S.A.

USA / Canada / UK / Ireland / Australia / New Zealand / India / South Africa / China
Penguin Books Ltd, Registered Offices: 80 Strand, London WC2R 0RL, England

For more information about the Penguin Group visit www.penguin.com

First published in the United States of America by Philomel Books,
a division of Penguin Young Readers Group, 2013
Published by Puffin Books, an imprint of Penguin Young Readers Group, 2013

Copyright © Shawn K. Stout, 2013

THE LIBRARY OF CONGRESS HAS CATALOGED THE PHILOMEL BOOKS EDITION AS FOLLOWS:
Stout, Shawn K.
Penelope Crumb never forgets / Shawn K. Stout. p. cm.—(Penelope Crumb ; 2)
Summary: During a fourth-grade field trip to Portwaller History Museum, Penelope fears that
she is losing her best friend, Patsy Cline Roberta Watson, and decides to start her own
secret museum so that she will never forget anyone important to her.
ISBN 978-0-399-25729-2 (hardcover)
[1. Museums—Fiction. 2. Best friends—Fiction. 3. Friendship—Fiction. 4. Behavior—Fiction.
5. Family life—Fiction. 6. School field trips—Fiction.] I. Title.
PZ7.S88838Pf2013 [Fic]—dc23 2012005997

Puffin Books ISBN 978-0-14-751009-9

Edited by Jill Santopolo. Design by Semadar Megged.

Printed in the United States of America

1 3 5 7 9 10 8 6 4 2

The publisher does not have any control over and does not assume any responsibility
for author or third-party websites or their content.

For my sister

PENELOPE CRUMB NEVER FORGETS

1.

Besides Miss Stunkel's art class, there's only one other thing I like about fourth grade. Field trips. Miss Stunkel calls them Outings for Educational Purposes, but I don't care what they are called as long as we get to be out of school and don't have to learn about decimal points.

The Educational Purpose for today's field trip is to learn about the history of Portwaller and not to goof off or act like chuckleheads. Which is what Miss Stunkel tells us a hundred times from the front of the bus. She stands up for the whole trip, stroking her Friday lizard pin with its ruby eyes and waiting for one of us to give her the chance to holler. Because that is what she likes to do most of all.

While she's doing all that standing, I notice that her feet aren't behind the yellow line, even though there's a sign above the bus driver's head that says FOR SAFETY, KEEP BEHIND THE YELLOW LINE WHEN BUS IS IN MOTION.

"Why doesn't Miss Stunkel sit down?" I say to my best friend, Patsy Cline Roberta Watson. "Mr. Drather should remind her. Maybe I should remind Mr. Drather."

Patsy Cline tells me to be quiet and that Mr. Drather doesn't have time to monitor the yellow line while he's concentrating on driving the bus. "You'll get in trouble. Remember what happened the last time," she says.

She means when we were on our last Outing for Educational Purposes at Fort McHenry. I was taking the steps at the fort two at a time even though they were big ones, and Miss Stunkel yelled,

"Penelope Crumb, the railings are there for a reason! I'm not going to tell you again!" Even though 1) she didn't need to yell and 2) she shouldn't have said "again," because that was really the first time she told me. But if I held on to the railings, I would be stuck behind slow people like Vera Bogg, who doesn't know how to have fun on stairs, so I pretended I didn't hear Miss Stunkel. I'm an excellent pretender.

"That's exactly what I mean," I say to Patsy Cline. "It's not my fault Miss Stunkel tried to catch up with me and fell down the stairs and sprained her knee."

Patsy Cline shakes her head at me. "You and Miss Stunkel are just like candy corn and corn chowder. You're both corn, but together you don't go down so easy."

"I'm just trying to look out for her safety," I say.

Patsy gives me a look that says, You're Going to Get Another Note Sent Home.

Good gravy. So I don't say anything to Mr.

Drather, because if Miss Stunkel doesn't know that there are seats on the bus for a reason, then I guess I'm not going to be the one to tell her.

Mr. Drather steers the bus into the parking lot behind the museum and turns off the engine. There's a lot of commotion when everybody stands up because we're tired of being cooped up in a school bus and are ready to look at all kinds of dead people's stuff. Which is what museums are full of.

I grab my red toolbox and nudge Patsy Cline toward the aisle.

Miss Stunkel says, "Everyone freeze!"

The bus gets quiet right away. Patsy Cline always follows directions, so she stops like she's been blasted with an ice machine, with one foot in the air. But her other foot doesn't freeze so well, because it's getting all wobbly, and I'm afraid she might go right down, so I grab on to her arm and pull. (Because that's what best friends do.)

Except that I guess I must have bigger muscles than I think, because Patsy comes tumbling right

into me. And when she does, she knocks me backward against the window. When that happens, I let go of my toolbox, and it hits the edge of the seat and falls to the floor.

I don't know what the floor of the bus is made out of, but when the metal from my toolbox hits it, there's an awful sound. For some reason, Miss Stunkel looks right at me and Patsy Cline. I put a look on my face that says, I Heard It Too, But I Don't Know Where It Came From. But that doesn't work, because Miss Stunkel gives me a look that says, Who Do You Think You're Fooling, Girlie?

Then Miss Stunkel clears her throat and says, "The Portwaller History Museum is a place of business, and I'm counting on each one of you to be on your best behavior." She pulls out her hand from the pocket of her corduroy jumper and holds up a finger in a warning.

I know that finger. I've seen it up close. It's scrawny except for the knuckles, kind of like a chicken leg that's been boiled, chewed on, and then dipped in orange nail polish.

"Because if you aren't on your best behavior," she says, still looking at me and Patsy Cline, "you will have the pleasure of spending the rest of the day on the bus."

Miss Stunkel is really good at making field trips seem like no fun at all.

Patsy Cline is still frozen even after Miss Stunkel finally tells us we can get off the bus. "It's okay, you can unfreeze now," I say to her. But she doesn't move. "What's the matter?"

"What did you pull me for?" she says. And her words have rocks in them.

"I thought you were going to fall."

"You *made* me fall," she says. "And we got into trouble."

"We didn't get into trouble." Getting into trouble with Miss Stunkel is a lot worse than just seeing her finger. And then I remember that Patsy Cline doesn't ever get into trouble, with Miss Stunkel or anybody else, so she wouldn't know what real trouble looks like. I tell her I'm sorry for pulling on her arm, but she just says "humph" and then nothing else.

We're the last ones into the museum. The Portwaller History Museum has got high ceilings with paintings on them, swirly things that turn into flowers that turn back into swirly things again. I could stare at them all day. And I would, too, except after a while, I get a crick in my neck, and when I finally look down again, I'm a little dizzy. My legs move sideways when they're supposed to go frontways, and before I can get control over them, I walk smack into Vera Bogg. Her bony elbow gets me right in the stomach.

Vera, who is always dressed head to toenail in pink, the kind of pink that makes me feel like a raw hot dog and also a baby pig with a temperature, moans and grabs her leg like she's hurt, even though I don't see how she could be. I tell her I'm sorry anyway and explain about the swirls.

Patsy Cline says, "You should watch where you're going." And at first I think she's talking to Vera, but then she pats Vera on the shoulder and asks her if she's okay. That's when I know she was talking to me.

Well, then.

After Vera limps away, I bring my shoulder over to Patsy, because if she's giving out shoulder pats, then I should get one, too. Seeing how I'm her best friend and all.

But I don't get one.

Instead, Patsy turns away from me and joins everybody else from our class hovering over a glass display case.

I squeeze in beside her and have a look. The first thing I see is a comb with one gray hair sticking in it that belonged to Maynard C. Portwaller. He's the dead guy who discovered our town and decided to name it after himself. Portwaller. That's what the card beside the comb says.

I shift my toolbox to my other hand and press

my face against the glass display case. I stare at the only thing left of Maynard C. Portwaller. "Did you know that hair keeps growing, even after you're dead?"

Everyone moans and grunts like I've said something gross. And then Miss Stunkel says, "That's *quite* enough, Penelope," making a big deal out of the *quite*. She doesn't like me talking about dead things. But I'm not very good at not talking about them. I guess it's because I have a dad who is Graveyard Dead and a grandpa who I thought was Graveyard Dead but turned out not to be.

And how am I supposed to not talk about dead things when there's a whole lot of dead-people stuff staring me right in the face? This is what I decide to ask Miss Stunkel after we're done looking at the gray hair from Maynard C. Portwaller (who also happens to be . . .).

But Miss Stunkel says, "Don't push me, Penelope Crumb."

And I say, "I would never do that, Miss Stunkel. You might fall down and sprain your knee."

Then Miss Stunkel gives me a look like she would very much like to push *me*. Right off a cliff.

Between Miss Stunkel and Patsy Cline, so far this Outing for Educational Purposes isn't going so good. I might as well be learning about decimal points.

2.

The first mayor of Portwaller, Charles Luckett," says Miss Stunkel, pointing to a painting of a man with a tall brown hat and round, wire-framed glasses. I get real close to have a look at his nose. This is something I like to do because I, Penelope Crumb, have a very big nose that I got from my grandpa Felix.

Mayor Luckett's nose isn't a big one. It's short and flat, and small for his head. Sort of like his nose stayed behind in fourth grade while the rest of his face grew up and went to college. But his nose is the *only* small thing about him. If Mister Leonardo da Vinci (who is my all-time favorite dead artist) were here, he'd surely say, "I don't believe I've ever seen such hardworking buttons on a shirt. The fine mayor looks to be the kind of man who is very fond of strawberry tarts."

I wonder if Mayor Luckett was proud of his big belly or if he thought the painter should have made him look a little skinnier. When I grow up and am a real famous artist person, I'm going to draw people just as they are: big bellies, big noses, and all.

A small wooden shelf sits right beside the painting of Mayor Luckett, and on that shelf, perched on a velvet cushion, are a pair of glasses that look just like the ones in the painting.

"These can't be his real, actual glasses," says Angus Meeker.

"Why not?" I say.

"Because he would have been wearing his real, actual glasses when he died."

Angus doesn't know anything about dead people. "Not if he died in his sleep," I say. "Therefore, he wouldn't." (*Therefore* is a new word I learned from my grandpa Felix. He's always teaching me new things.)

Miss Stunkel gives me a look that says, I've Heard Enough Out of You, Penelope Crumb. Therefore, Be Quiet. Then she says to the whole class that indeed they are Mayor Luckett's actual glasses and that they were loaned to the museum by his family.

"Will his family ever get his glasses back?" I ask.

"They still belong to the mayor's family," Miss Stunkel says. "The glasses just live at the museum now because the family wanted the citizens of Portwaller to be able to see them anytime they wish."

I tighten the grip on my toolbox. It belonged to my dad, who is Graveyard Dead, and I know I could never let any museum have it. Not even his shoehorn, which is the only other thing I have that belonged to him. What if something happened to them?

And as if Miss Stunkel could read those very thoughts in my brain, she says, "A few years ago, the museum caught fire, and many treasured items, including some of the oldest pictures of Portwaller, were lost."

"You mean, gone forever?" I say.

Miss Stunkel touches her Friday lizard pin. "Nothing could be done to save them, I'm afraid. But thanks to the donations from some very generous Portwallerians, the building has been repaired. You may have noticed the donation box when we came in."

I hug the toolbox to my chest and wish that gone forever didn't always mean gone forever.

"Let's keep going," says Miss Stunkel, rubbing her hands together. "We want to save some time for the gift shop!"

Next on display is a pair of shoes, a rusty key that's as big as my hand, and a broken dinner plate.

Each one has a tiny card in front of it that tells you how old it is and why it is important enough to be in a museum. Here's what they say:

WOMEN'S SHOES, CIRCA 1889.

KEY TO PORTWALLER JAIL, 1911.

PLATE BELONGING TO FAMILY OF WALTER
P. FINNBROOK. THOUGHT TO HAVE
BEEN USED BY THOMAS JEFFERSON,
THE THIRD PRESIDENT OF THE UNITED
STATES, DURING A GRAND PARTY AT THE
FINNBROOK ESTATE, CIRCA 1819.

I slide my hand along the glass display cases, studying everything in them and trying to imagine the people they belonged to. In the next case are baby clothes that the card says are more than a hundred years old. Next to that, a teddy bear that's missing both eyeballs, one ear, and some fur, and generally looks an awful mess, not too different from Patsy Cline's dog, Roger, last summer when he came down with mange.

I can't help but wonder what happened to that baby and why she left that mangy teddy behind. And how did the museum come to get it, anyway? I squeeze the handle of my toolbox a little tighter.

"Where are the rest of the baby's clothes and toys?" I ask. "What happened to them?"

But Miss Stunkel and everyone else in my class, including Patsy Cline, have moved on and left me and Mangy Teddy alone with all the other dead people's stuff. The room is quiet. Dead quiet. Even without eyeballs, that teddy is giving me a look that says, Where Did Everybody Go?

There's a whole row of display cases that we haven't even gotten to yet. Full of things—special and important things, probably—that belonged to real people. People who everybody has forgotten about. And here's something else I know: When you forget about dead people, it's like they were never really here at all.

I march into the museum gift shop, where I find the rest of my class. A couple of boys are stabbing each other with toy Civil War bayonets. Others are trying to decide between a glow-in-the-dark card deck and a Portwaller Town Hall jigsaw puzzle. Angus Meeker is playing with a tall brown hat that looks like the kind Mayor Luckett was wearing in the painting.

And Miss Stunkel (Miss Stunkel!) is trying on umbrellas.

I can feel my ears start to sweat. "What's the matter with you all? We didn't finish looking at all the stuff in there!" I yell, pointing to the museum room.

Everybody stops. My words are a heavy blanket, one that has been kept in the corner of a basement and smells of mold. It covers the room and ruins everybody's good fun.

Miss Stunkel grips the umbrella and then peers at me out of the corners of her eyeballs. She's got a look on her face that says, Ready, Aim, Fire! But instead of hurling the umbrella at me, she just holds her chicken-bone finger in the air.

I nod to let her know I don't want any trouble. After a long moment, she tucks her finger back inside her jumper pocket and slides the umbrella into the wooden barrel with all the others. Then she turns away from me to keep from having murdering thoughts.

I turn away, too, and that's when I see Patsy Cline and Vera Bogg side by side at the jewelry counter, with their shoulders touching and their heads entirely too close together.

I wriggle between them, pushing them apart. "Everybody left me behind in there." I point to the museum room. "There's more to see, you know. Things that are more important than a gift shop."

"Sorry," says Patsy Cline.

But she doesn't look sorry. And I'm about to tell her so when Vera dangles a small white sand dollar swinging from a chain in front of my nose. Engraved on it in deep letters are the words FRIENDS FOREVER. "Look what we got," Vera says.

"We who?" And then I see the same necklace peeking out from underneath Patsy Cline's frizzy hair.

Good gravy.

Before I can help myself, right then and there in the museum gift shop, I open my mouth as wide as it will go. And then I yell loud enough for even one-eared, Mangy Teddy to hear. "Doesn't anybody care about dead people? Dead people are people, too!" And then I reach into my pockets, pull out all the money that I had emptied from my piggy bank that morning—fifteen dollars and fourteen cents, plus a Canadian penny—and find the museum's donation box. "This," I announce as I stuff the money into the slot, "is for dead people everywhere!"

3.

M r. Drather swings open the door to the bus and says, "Back so soon?"

I climb inside and slide into my seat. He's got the radio on a country-western music station, and there's a man singing some sad song about good love gone bad.

He turns around in his seat. "Didn't learn anything from the Fort McHenry incident, did you, kid?"

"No."

"Guess not." He unwraps a candy bar and breaks

it in half before eating it. "Mary hurt again this time?"

"Mary who?" I say.

He picks at the corners of his mouth with his thumbnail. "Sorry. Miss Stunkel, I mean."

My word. I didn't even know that Miss Stunkel had a first name. "Miss Stunkel's name is Mary? She doesn't really look like a Mary."

"What does a Mary look like?" he says.

"First of all," I say, "a Mary doesn't have a mean face, like she's sucking on lemon seeds all the time. And she has nice eyes. The kind that when they look at you don't wish you were dead."

He must not know what to say to that, because he turns around in his seat and taps his fingers on the steering wheel.

I take out my drawing pad from my toolbox and draw a Mary who is not Miss Stunkel. When I finish, I take it to the front of the bus and show Mr. Drather.

"You draw pretty good," he says.

"Want me to draw you?"

He shrugs. "Do I have to do anything more than what I'm doing right now?"

I say, "What are you doing right now?"

"Nothing," he says.

And I tell him that's just fine. I sit cross-legged on the floor by his seat and start drawing his wavy brown hair that's real short on top and on the sides and real long in the back. "How much longer do you think they are going to be?"

"Who?" he says.

"You know, Mary. And the rest of my class."

"Now, don't you go calling her Mary," he says. "She's Miss Stunkel to you."

"Okay, fine. When do you think Miss Stunkel and everybody else will be done in there?"

"Don't know. A while more, I'd say."

I get back to my drawing. "You've got a real nice round nose."

"Think so?" He sniffs the air. "It's been working all right for me so far."

"That's good." I get to his chin, which has a big

pucker in it. Like someone finger-poked a mound of wet clay and let it dry. I'm about to tell him this, but a song I know starts playing on the radio. "Patsy Cline!"

Mr. Drather gets a smile on his face that says, Thank You, Lord Above. And his chin pucker almost disappears. He turns up the volume to the radio. "How do you know Patsy Cline?"

I tell him how my best friend, Patsy Cline Roberta Watson, is named after Patsy Cline the dead country-western singer. And how Patsy Cline, my best friend, is also a singer who knows how to sing songs by Patsy Cline, the dead one. "Did you know she is dead?"

He nods. "I did." Then he tells me that if I could be quiet for a minute, we might actually be able to hear her sing.

I keep on drawing while the song plays, and Mr. Drather even sings along in a couple of parts.

I've got your picture that you gave to me,
And it's signed "with love," just like it used to be.
The only thing different, the only thing new,

I've got your picture, she's got you.

He's not as good of a singer as Patsy Cline (either one), but he's not the worst I've ever heard. One time I sat outside our bathroom listening to my brother, Terrible, sing in the shower. Do all aliens sound like roosters that have just had their tonsils taken out? Which is what I asked Terrible when he caught me listening. But he just punched me in the arm and I never heard him sing again.

After the song is over, Mr. Drather turns down the volume and sings the last verse again real loud. Then he stares out the front window of the bus for a long while.

I whisper, "Mr. Drather?"

Then he jumps a little like he's forgotten he's sitting inside a school bus. And that I'm here with him. His face turns red, all except for his chin pucker. "Right. Sorry."

"That's okay." I decide to put a stage and a curtain and a microphone in my drawing, along with lots of musical notes. When I'm finished, I show him the drawing.

He doesn't say anything at first, only takes in a deep breath and holds it. Then he touches one of the music notes with his fingertip.

"Well?" I say. "Do you like it? I put you on a stage. You know, because it seems to me that you like to sing."

"I see that." He clears his throat. "And I do."

I tear off the page and hand it to him. "Here. You can have it, if you want."

He nods at me and smiles. Then he rolls up the drawing, pulls a rubber band from around his wrist, and slides it over the drawing. With both hands, he tucks it into a bag by his seat. "So you never did say why you're here."

"What do you mean?" I say.

He jabs his thumb in the direction of the museum. "I mean, what did you do this time to get into trouble?"

"Oh, that," I say. "I yelled and caused a disruption that interfered with our learning." Which is how Miss Stunkel put it before she told me I'd earned an afternoon on the bus.

Mr. Drather raises his eyebrows at me.

So I tell him that all everybody was doing was fooling around in the gift shop anyway, which doesn't involve any learning, so my yelling couldn't have gotten in the way of that.

"What did you go and yell for in the first place?"

"Because there was stuff in the museum that we skipped over," I say. "Don't you think we should remember those people?"

He shrugs. "I've never been much for museums myself. But I think there are plenty of people we should remember, even if their stuff doesn't make it into a museum." He pulls at his long hair. "But that's why you yelled for real?"

I nod. "And also Patsy and Vera and their matching necklaces."

Mr. Drather folds his arms across his chest. "Sounds to me like maybe you're the one that was skipped over."

And when I think about Patsy Cline, I think maybe he's right.

4.

Miss Stunkel sends a note home. It's the fifth one this year, but I'm hoping my mom isn't keeping track.

I don't have to read the note in order to know what it says.

Dear Mrs. Crumb,

Penelope just can't seem to be able to keep her mouth shut. Especially when it comes to talking about dead things. Please see what you can do to keep her quiet in my

class. Or else I may have to kill her with an
umbrella.

Sincerely,
Miss Stunkel, who is a mean Mary

When I pull the envelope from my tool-box, my mom shakes her head and gives me a look that says, What Am I Going to Do With You? So I answer, "Get me a new fourth-grade teacher."

She must not know what to say about that, because she puts her feet in our broken dryer, which she uses as a desk, and then stares off at the new drawing she's working on. Mom draws pictures of people's insides for books that doctors read. And this one is on brains.

I prop myself up against our washing machine next to her. "Is that what my brains look like? They have a lot of wrinkles."

"Penelope Rae." She has a way of saying my

name like it's one of the gross insides she draws. (Brain wrinkles, for example.)

I change the subject. "Did you know that the Portwaller History Museum caught on fire and some of the stuff in it burned all up?"

Mom is still reading Miss Stunkel's note, so all she says is "humph" and then nothing else.

"Can I borrow fifteen dollars?"

That gets her attention. She stops reading and says, "Not on your life."

"Why not?"

She says, "There are so many reasons why I shouldn't give you fifteen dollars, I want to hear a reason why I should."

"Because I want to buy something at the Port-waller History Museum. A necklace."

She waves the note at me. "According to this, you were there today. Why didn't you just buy it then? Too busy getting into trouble, I guess." She folds up the note and sticks it back into the enve-lope. "Where's all your money?"

But before I can tell her I gave it all to the museum, an alien attack is launched against me. From behind, Terrible flicks my ears, and when I lift up my hands to cover them, he gets me in my armpits. "Yeeow!"

Soon after my brother, Terrence, turned fourteen, he was snatched by aliens. The aliens returned him, but when they did, he wasn't the same. He was Terrible. I've already written a letter to NASA about his alien ways, but until they write back, all I can do is keep a close watch on him.

Mom says, "Leave your sister alone."

This is impossible for aliens to do.

"Have you seen my gray jacket?" he asks, flicking me again.

"I washed it," says Mom. "It's drying on the balcony."

"You washed it! What for?" (Here's a fact: Aliens like to smell bad.) Terrible gives my ears another flick and then steps over the piles of Mom's schoolbooks and onto our tiny porch.

Mom slides a drawing pencil behind her ear and fingers Miss Stunkel's note. "We'll talk about this more after we meet with your teacher."

"What do you mean? Why do we have to meet with her?" I take the note out of her hand and read it. The note doesn't say anything about killing me with an umbrella, but it does say she wants to talk about my behavior. I keep reading.

"Hold the phone," I say when I get to the part where Miss Stunkel says I often "exhibit odd behavior." Odd? It's not like I eat paste or dip my food in applesauce. "I don't even like apple-sauce!" I announce. "And, cross my heart and hope to die, I haven't eaten any glue since the time Angus Meeker bet me two dollars I didn't have the guts!"

Mom tells me to hold it together and that she's sure Miss Stunkel doesn't think of me that way—as truly odd.

I say, "You don't know Miss Stunkel."

She says, "I guess I will have to get to know her, then."

Which is not the best thing to hear your mom say.

On the way to my room, I'm wondering how I'm going to get out of this one when Littie Maple almost hits me with the door to our apartment. "Can I watch TV?" she says, barreling past me toward our couch. "Oh, yeah, and my momma wants me to ask if she can borrow an egg. She's making a frittata for World Egg Day and needs six eggs but only has five. And take your time getting it, because *Max Adventure* is on."

"For someone who doesn't have a TV, you sure are an expert about what's on."

Littie smiles at me like I just gave her a kitten-shaped lollipop. I put my toolbox on the counter and grab an egg from the refrigerator. I cup it with both hands and take it to her.

"I said go slow," she says. "Max hasn't seen the Great Serpent of Hootcheekoo Creek yet!"

"What's that around your neck?"

Littie holds out a black box hung on a strap. "It's an alarm. Momma is letting me have more adventures now, but I have to wear this."

"How does it work?"

"I just pull this thing," she says, grabbing the black box. She pulls, and WONK!! WONK!! WONK!! WONK!! WONK!! WONK!!

"Littie!"

She plugs the black box back into the strap and the WONK! stops. "It's a little loud."

"A little."

From out of nowhere, Terrible pops me on the back of my head. "Where's the fire?"

"That was just Littie's neck alarm," I say.

He puts on his jacket while making a face at me and then says, "Later, wombat." Then he pulls on Littie's ponytail and heads out the door.

Littie's eyeballs are now stuck in his direction. "Where do you think he's going?"

"Don't know," I say, holding out the egg to her. "Don't care." But she doesn't see me.

"He didn't even say good-bye."

"What are you even talking about, Littie Maple?" But her brains are someplace else.

I get tired of holding the egg and decide to see

if it can fit in my mouth. It can. I tap Littie on the head to get her attention.

Littie finally looks at me. She shakes her head. "You wouldn't do that if you knew where eggs came from. I'm just saying."

I pull the egg out of my mouth and wipe it with my shirtsleeve. "For your information, I do know where eggs come from."

Littie gives me a look that says, Then You Are One Weird Tomato.

Which makes me wonder. "Do you think I'm odd?"

"Sure thing." Littie's eyes are back on the TV.

"No, I mean *weird* odd."

"Definitely."

"Littie!"

"You just put an egg in your mouth, even when you knew it came out of a chicken's backside."

"I was trying to get your attention," I say. "Besides, they wash the eggs before they get to the grocery store."

"Who does?"

"You know, the egg people," I say. "The people in charge of the eggs."

Littie laughs and shakes her head. Then she says, "Don't worry, Penelope, weird doesn't bother me. I'm just saying."

Which makes me wonder if maybe weird bothers Patsy Cline.

5.

Grandpa Felix hollers at me to keep up. "Get the lead out!" His camera bags strung across my back are heavy, and my feet keep slipping on the wet grass. Piney Hill is steep and good for sledding, but I can't figure why anybody would want to have a wedding on top of it.

"Why do you need so many?" I ask, taking bigger steps to catch up.

He turns his head to the side. "So many what?"

I grunt out, "Cameras."

"You might as well ask me why I need so many friends," he says. "No such thing as too many."

The strap of one bag slides off my shoulder and down my arm. I sling it back up, but I can tell it's not going to stay put. I shift my toolbox to my other hand. "Well, your friends sure are heavy."

"You're young," he says. "Hard work makes your cheeks rosy. You want rosy cheeks, don't you?"

"Not really," I say.

"Well, you should." He slows for a second and looks at me over his shoulder. "And you should have left that toolbox in the truck like I told you."

I tighten my grip. "You couldn't leave any of *your* friends behind."

He laughs and says, "I guess not," and then speeds ahead.

By the time I catch up, Grandpa is at the top of the hill under a big white tent. I let the camera bags fall from my shoulders, and I sink to the ground. The wet grass is soaking through my skirt, but I'm too out of breath from the climb to care.

"Up and at 'em," Grandpa says. "I can't have

an assistant with wet drawers. Unpack my cameras while I have a talk with the people in charge."

"Aren't you tired?" I say. "Don't you want to take a rest?"

"I am not," he says, pulling me to my feet. "There's plenty of time to rest when I'm dead."

I unzip the bags, carefully pull out Grandpa's cameras by the straps, and hang all three of them around my neck. Then I pull at the back of my wet pants to unstick them.

While I wait for Grandpa, the empty white tent fills up with rows of wooden fold-up chairs, dangly streamers, and flowers in purple and yellow bunches. By the time Grandpa returns to me, a wedding day has sprung up right in front of us, like from the pages of a pop-up book.

"We're going to start over here," he tells me, pointing to the stone path behind us. "This way." He presses his hand on my shoulder and leads me down the path along a row of pine trees. "Now, you've got to stick close so I can switch cameras when I need to. Got it?"

"Can I take some pictures, too?"

"No, ma'am. Not today."

"When can I?"

"Some other time," he says.

"You always say that."

"Then it must be true." He takes one camera from around my neck and holds it up to his eyeball. "Besides, this isn't the kind of camera you're used to."

While Grandpa has his face pressed up against the camera, a white-haired man in a black suit comes over and taps him on the shoulder. "Felix Crumb," he says.

"That's me," says Grandpa, without looking at the man.

"I'd recognize that nose anywhere." He sticks out his hand.

Grandpa Felix tucks the camera under his arm and shakes the man's hand. He doesn't let go, not for a long time. He stares into the man's eyes like he's looking on a map for the next turn. Finally from somewhere hidden in one of his brain wrinkles, Grandpa Felix remembers. "I don't believe it," he says.

"It's been forty years, and you've still got a camera in your hand," says the man.

"Mandrake Trout," says Grandpa.

"Mandrake?" I say. Because it sounds more like a kind of long-legged bird than a person's name.

Grandpa squeezes my shoulder. "This is my Penelope. I mean, she's my granddaughter."

"I see the resemblance," he says. And I know he means my nose. I flare my nostrils at him. Twice. Mandrake smiles at me and says, "How do you do?"

I tell him that I do just fine.

Then he's back to Grandpa. "I can't believe it," he says, knocking him in the shoulder. "Still a shutterbug, eh? Is that the same Leica Rangefinder?" He grabs the camera from Grandpa and puts it up to his eyeball.

"Right," says Grandpa, pulling on the camera strap until Mandrake lets go.

Mandrake says, "Same old Felix, stuck in the past." He puts his hands on his knees and bends down so his face is right at mine. "Penelope, your granddad and I grew up together. Stickball, Maryland's Young Explorers, summer camp at Deep Creek Lake, Photography Club." He looks at the cameras around my neck. "So, he's roped you into this nonsense gig?"

I don't know what that means, so I just nod and shrug. Which seems to work okay, because he goes on about how his niece is getting married to some big-shot newspaper man, and that he's only in town for a couple of days.

Grandpa moves a piece of tree bark along the edge of a stone with his shoe. He nods along, but he seems a lot more interested in the tree bark than, what Mandrake has to say. And he has a lot to say.

"So let's catch up before I leave," Mandrake says. Then he hands Grandpa a card with his name and phone number on it. He pats me on the head like I'm a stray dog that needs a bath. I want to bite him. He tells me it was nice talking with me. Even though he's the one who did all the talking.

"Mandrake," I say, after he's gone. It gets caught on my tongue. "Mandrake."

"Yep," says Grandpa.

"Mandrake. Man. Drake. Mannnnd. Raaaake."

"Penelope."

"Sorry. I never met any of your friends before," I say. "Except for Mr. Caldenia, who lives in your building and always asks me if it's going to rain."

"I haven't thought about Mandrake Trout in years."

"He sure did remember your camera," I say.

Grandpa tightens his grip like he's holding on to something more than just a camera. "This is a thirty-five-millimeter Leica Rangefinder. This one uses actual film."

"Oh."

"The same kind that Eisenstaedt used," he says. "I don't expect you know who Eisenstaedt is."

"Sure I do," I say. "The really smart old guy with funny white hair."

Grandpa Felix shakes his head and tells me Eisenstaedt, not Einstein. But when I give him a look that says, What's the Difference? he says, "Alfred Eisenstaedt was a photographer. *Albert Einstein* was a physicist. Both were geniuses."

"Were?"

"Yes, Penelope," he says, "they're both long dead. The point is, you know how you feel about Leonardo da Vinci? That's how I feel about Eisenstaedt. Get it?"

"Got it."

He turns the camera over in his hand. "This was my very first. I bought it at Driscoll's flea market with the money I saved from delivering newspapers. Still works like a charm." He looks through the viewfinder at the sky and then at the trees behind me. "They don't make them like this anymore."

"We should name it," I say. "Let's call it Alfred. After, you know, the guy."

"Eisenstaedt."

"Yeah, him."

Grandpa Felix says, "Whatever you say."

"Maybe it will be in a museum someday," I say.

"What will?"

"Alfred. So that people will remember you. And know that you took very nice pictures."

"What means something to me isn't going to be worth the dirt we're standing on to anybody else long after I'm gone." He points the camera at me and presses the button until it clicks.

I bet Maynard C. Portwaller never thought his gray hair would be on display for everyone to see. But it is. And people must think that one piece of hair is worth more than the dirt we're standing on if it's in a museum. I tell Grandpa Felix this, but all he says is, "I'm no Maynard C. Portwaller."

"That's right," I tell him. "You're Grandpa Felix Crumb. And I'll remember you long after you're gone. And when I'm a famous artist, people will see my drawings and remember me long after I'm Graveyard Dead. Just like Mister Leonardo da Vinci."

Grandpa raises his eyebrows at me. "You know, you probably shouldn't be wasting your Saturday with an old man like me when you could be having some fun with Patsy Cline."

What I don't say is how Patsy Cline is probably already having fun with Vera Bogg. Here's what I do say: "This is fun, Grandpa."

He shakes his head. "Well, I'm glad you think so."

"Do you know what would make it even more fun?" I say. "If you let me take some pictures."

"Nice try." He walks along the stone path toward the pine trees. "This way. Let's get this over with."

I grab the camera bags and sling them over my shoulder. "How come you haven't thought about Mandrake for so long?"

He shrugs. "I don't know. I just haven't."

"But you were friends?"

He nods. "The best."

"Then why?"

"Nothing is forever. You'll learn that someday."

I say, "Some things are." Like my dad being gone forever. And what about what's on Patsy's and Vera's necklaces? FRIENDS FOREVER.

"Sometimes you forget about things or people that seemed really important long ago." He holds Alfred up to his face.

"I won't," I say. "I don't want to forget."

6.

What are you doing in there?" asks Littie Maple.

I stick my head out from inside my closet. "Nothing." I throw the last of my shoes and hang-up clothes onto the Heap. Which now comes up to Littie's eyeballs.

"It doesn't look like nothing." Littie grabs my pair of my polka-dotted rain boots from the Heap and holds them up to her feet. She tells me I must be related to Sasquatch and then throws the boots back on the pile. She finds a pair of my sandals and buckles them over her socks. "Can I have these," she asks, "if you're going to throw them out?"

"I'm not throwing them out," I tell her.

"Oh." Littie clunks over to my dresser and kicks up her leg to try to get a look at her foot in the mirror. "I really like them. I'm just saying. And they fit me perfect."

I give Littie a look that says, That's a Good One. But I don't say anything about the sandals, because if she doesn't know she has tiny bird feet, then I'm not going to be the one to tell her.

"Is your brother at home?" asks Littie.

"I hope not."

"Remember the other day when he pulled my hair?" she says, standing on her tiptoes.

"I don't know. I guess."

"Remember? We were out there by the couch and he was going somewhere, because he just put his jacket on and he said something to you and then he pulled on my hair? Remember?"

I shrug and push some of my clothes and shoes to the top of the Heap.

"I mean, on a regular day, he usually pays no attention to me at all. Doesn't even say hello or anything. But the other day, he pulled my hair . . . You really don't remember?" she says, folding her arms across her chest. But when I don't answer, she says, "*I* do. I remember."

"You can tell Mom if you want," I say. "Terrible pulls my hair and does worse to me all the time and hardly ever gets into trouble, but maybe if you told Mom, she would do something."

"I don't want to get him into trouble," she says, and her face turns red. "That's not what I'm after."

"Then what?"

"Nothing, Penelope," she says. "Nothing."

"Why are you so bothered about Terrible, anyway?"

She unbuckles my sandals and kicks them off. "Never mind."

I crawl into my empty closet, curl into a corner, and run my hand over the white walls. If Mister Leonardo da Vinci were here, he would surely say, "My goodness, thank lucky stars for such a place as this. Oh me, oh my, indeed the plain walls should not be plain for long." Because that is how dead artists talk.

Littie clucks her tongue like a pigeon from the other side of the Heap. And then maybe because sitting in an empty closet makes my brains work better, all of a sudden it hits me why Littie is so bothered about Terrible. I grab a shoe from the bottom of the Heap and throw it at her. My aim must be pretty good, because she lets out a yowl. "What the heck did you do that for?"

"Because, Littie Maple, if you're meaning to say that you like Terrible the space alien, blech, then maybe you're an alien, too." I crawl back into my closet and prop my feet against the wall.

"What are you doing in there?"

"Nothing," I say.

Her clucks get louder. "Well, what are you doing with all this stuff out here? And don't say 'nothing.'"

"I just don't want it in my closet."

"Why not?" she says.

I sigh. "Because."

"Because why?"

"My closet isn't going to be a closet anymore, that's why."

"What's it going to be?"

I can almost hear Leonardo say, "I am simply unable to think with all this clucking in my ears. Thank lucky stars that this wonderful room has a door."

I tell Littie that I don't know what it's going to be.

"You don't know?" she says. I bet she's got her hands on her hips now. "Penelope Crumb, if you don't want to tell me what you're doing, then just say you don't want to tell me instead of saying you don't know. Because if you—"

"Okay, Littie," I say. "I don't really want to tell you."

"You don't want to tell me!" she yells. "Well, that's just a bruise on a banana, isn't it! Why? Why don't you want to—"

I close the closet door then, and the clucking stops soon after. "Ah, how lovely and quiet when the pigeon leaves the windowsill," Leonardo would say. "Now, let's get to thinking. Whose things are you going to put in this wonderful museum of yours?"

7.

I call Patsy Cline the next day. "Do you want to come over?"

"It's Sunday," she says. "I've got practice."

"Oh, right," I say. "I forgot." I tap my brains to wake them up. "Maybe I could come over, then?"

Patsy doesn't say anything. But I can tell she's still there because I can hear her mom in the background calling her to come finish her scrambled eggs. "I guess that would be okay," she says finally.

I hang up the phone and yell to Mom, "I'm going over to Patsy Cline's!"

Patsy lives two metro stops away. On the train, I flip the handle of my toolbox back and forth, while my stomach does some flipping of its own. "I hope I'm not getting the stomach flu," I tell my stomach. The man sitting next to me says, "I hope not, too," and then he changes seats.

When I finally get to Patsy's building, my stomach is making all kinds of noises, and I'm worried the elevator might not be fast enough. But then as I'm getting ready to knock on Patsy's door, my heart is really pounding, and I know that what I have isn't the flu: It's nerves.

I don't know why I would be nervous about visiting Patsy Cline, whom I have visited more times than I can count, but I take a deep breath and try to slow my heart. Then I knock.

Patsy Cline's dog, Roger, barks and scratches at the door. I can hear Patsy tell Roger to keep it down, and then the door opens. There's Patsy in her blue cowgirl outfit with Roger tucked under her arm. "Howdy," she says.

As soon as I see her, my nerves go away, but then I see her FRIENDS FOREVER necklace around her neck, and my stomach does another flip. It doesn't help that Roger, who has a face like a vampire bat and is missing a great number of his teeth, growls and lunges at me like he wants to gum me to death. With a face like that, Roger should thank lucky stars he doesn't have a tail, because if Patsy Cline hadn't adopted him, he'd still be at that shelter. Or worse.

"He's having one of his bad days," Patsy explains.

It's not easy being a dog when you're missing your tail, I guess. "I know the feeling," I say quietly, and follow her inside. Somehow between the knock and Roger's bad day, I decide the best thing to do is to keep talking and not let there be any empty space, because empty space will leave room for Vera Bogg. So right away I tell her about how Mr. Drather was singing a Patsy Cline song on the bus the day of the field trip and how I drew a picture of him and about how I think he wants to be a singer but is driving a school bus now instead. And how I had forgotten to tell her about that on the way home from the Portwaller History Museum on account of the fact that my brains were on Miss Stunkel and the note she sent home.

And then without giving that story a chance to settle, I start telling the one about Mandrake. But before I can even get to the part about Grandpa Felix's camera, the one we decided to name Alfred, Patsy's mom says from the other room, "Patsy, let's run through this song one more time."

"Hi, Mrs. Watson," I yell.

Patsy's mom says, "Honey child!" Patsy's mom always calls me honey child. And especially today it sounds so nice when she says it. A child made of honey. That's what she thinks of me. And then she says this: "You make yourself right at home, Vera. Patsy has just about got this song handled."

And that's when I just about go dead. I know I do, because all of a sudden, I can't feel my tongue, and I can't feel my toenails. And I wonder how long I have until my heart stops going.

Patsy Cline's face turns bright red. "It's not Vera," she yells to her mom. "It's Penelope."

"Oh, no matter," says her mom. As if Vera is also made out of honey. Which I know she definitely is not. Then Mrs. Watson tells me to make myself at home anyway. But she doesn't call me honey child. Not even once.

I wait for Patsy in her room. She's got shelves and shelves of trophies for singing, and a big poster of Patsy Cline, the dead country-western singer, above her bed. I plop down on her bed and close my eyes. I know this room by heart. With my eyes closed, I make a list from my memory of everything in the room.

Thirteen gold trophies, three silver ones, four blue ribbons, one red, a Patsy Cline poster, green bedspread with tiny yellow butterflies and curtains to match, yellow shaggy rug, white desk and chair, blue plastic bins filled with her cow collection, a keyboard with a microphone, and a lamp with a cow-print shade. Patsy Cline really likes cows.

I open my eyes and check my memory. Pretty good, except I forgot about the framed picture of me and Patsy on the roller coaster at FantasyLand last summer. And also there are fourteen gold trophies—somehow I missed one. I kneel on her bed and pull down the last trophy in the lineup. It's small, but heavy, and the gold part is in the shape of a music note. At the base, there's an engraving: PATSY CLINE ROBERTA WATSON. FIRST PLACE. PORTWALLER'S TALENTED VOICES.

I turn over the trophy in my hand and wonder if one day I will forget about Patsy Cline, about our trip to FantasyLand, about how much she likes cows. Just like how Grandpa one day stopped thinking about Mandrake Trout and then forgot all about him.

There is one way to make sure I don't forget. I open my toolbox and try to stuff the trophy inside. Only, it doesn't fit too good because of all the other stuff I keep in there. So I dump out my drawing pad and pencils, markers, shoehorn, flashlight, change purse, granola bar, and then try again. The top of the music note scrapes against the side of my toolbox. I push down the lid, but it won't close all the way.

As soon as I open the toolbox again to try one more time, Patsy Cline walks in singing, "Worry, why do I let myself worry? Wondering what in the world did I do?" Then she sees me stuffing her trophy into my toolbox and says, "What in the world?"

"Oh," I say, yanking the trophy out of my toolbox. I put it back on the shelf and tell Patsy that I was going to draw it while I waited for her to finish her singing practice and that I wanted to see if it would fit in my toolbox, just because. And then I say, "I can fit a whole egg in my mouth."

Patsy gives me a look that says, You Are Crazier Than Roger.

While I put all my things back in my toolbox, I change the subject. "Want to go to the park?"

"What for?" she says.

What for? I don't know what kind of a dumb question that is, because what does anybody go to the park for? But I don't say that because that's not the kind of thing you say to your best friend. Instead, I say, "To spin on the turnabout until we get so dizzy we can't walk straight."

Patsy Cline says, "No, thanks."

I tap my brains to get them going. "How about a staring contest?"

Patsy smiles, and then her eyes pop wide open. I'm an excellent starer. But Patsy is the All-Time Best, and she knows it. She can stare at you for so long that she doesn't even see you anymore, and she can keep on staring even after you've given up and gone home for supper. It's a little creepy, truth be told.

I set my eyes on her left eyebrow, which I named Marge because it looks like a caterpillar. I stare at Marge for a long time without blinking, seems like days. I stare so long and so hard that my eyes start to water, which is usually how it goes. Marge gets all blurry, and then it happens. I blink.

Patsy gets a big smile on her face, the kind of smile that makes me think we're still best friends, even if she is still wearing that necklace, and then she says, "Want to go again?"

8.

An empty museum is nothing more than a closet. This is what I tell Leonardo da Vinci while I sit in the dark. If he were really here, he would surely say, "A museum does not make itself."

"I tried to get Patsy Cline's trophy," I tell him. If only my toolbox were bigger. "Why do they have to make trophies so big, anyway?"

"I know nothing of trophies," he would say. "In my day, people did not get statuettes for singing, only for jousting. I should have liked to receive one for my paintings, I do believe."

"But I still don't know what to put in my museum."

"What you need, little darling, is what every artist needs. Some inspiration."

"Inspiration," I repeat.

The laundry room is where I find some. I pull a handful of drawing pencils and paintbrushes from the mason jars lined up on the dryer/desk and tuck them under my arm. Then I grab a couple tubes of paint—raw sienna, lemon yellow, and my favorite: ultramarine. I like to say it out loud. *Ultramarine. Ultramarine.* Because it's not just marine. It's *ultra* marine.

I stuff the tubes into my pocket.

When I turn around, there's the alien behind me. Aliens have the quietest footsteps, and you can't hear them coming. That makes them very good at the sneak attack.

"What are you doing?" says Terrible.

I answer with a question of my own. "What are *you* doing?"

He gives me a Hairy Eyeball, but I sidestep past him and head to my room before he can do any of his alien mind tricks on me.

I pull the paint tubes from my pockets, and I look at the white walls of my closet. Before this can really be a museum, it needs a name. I tap my head to get my brains started and then, after a while, I come up with one. Brain wrinkles are amazing things.

I paint in big *ultra*marine letters on the wall:

PENELOPE CRUMB'S ULTRA MUSEUM OF PEOPLE WHO WON'T BE FORGOTTEN EVEN AFTER THEY ARE GRAVEYARD DEAD

The letters go the whole way across the one wall and then turn the corner and go across the next one.

"That's a mouthful," Leonardo would say.

I make some changes.

PENELOPE CRUMB'S ULTRA MUSEUM
OF PEOPLE WHO ~~WON'T BE
FORGOTTEN EVEN AFTER THEY ARE
GRAVEYARD DEAD~~ SHOULDN'T BE
FORGOTTEN

PENELOPE CRUMB'S ULTRA MUSEUM
OF ~~PEOPLE WHO WON'T BE
FORGOTTEN EVEN AFTER THEY ARE
GRAVEYARD DEAD SHOULDN'T BE
FORGOTTEN~~ FORGET–ME–NOTTERS

I can practically hear Leonardo say, "Now *that* is ultra good."

And it is. Having a name is a good start, and while the paint dries, I get out my drawing pad and pencil and make a list of all the people I don't want to forget about:

> *Mom*
>
> *Grandpa Felix*
>
> *Dad*
>
> *Nanny and Pop-Pop*

Aunt Renn

Uncle Cleigh

Patsy Cline Roberta Watson

Terrence (my brother, not the alien)

Littie Maple

Penelope Crumb's Ultra Museum of Forget-Me-Notters doesn't have any glass display cases like the ones at the Portwaller History Museum, so a dinner plate from our kitchen cupboard will have to do. I pull out the first thing for my museum from my toolbox—my dad's shoehorn. It's silver metal and gleams except for the curved part in the center, where I imagine the rubbing of my dad's heel took the shine off. I look into the shiny part and can see some of me in the reflection.

I put the shoehorn on the plate and then slide it to the center of the floor. Then I make a card that says

Shoehorn that belonged to Theodore Crumb, dad to Penelope Crumb, and who is Graveyard Dead.

9.

At school the next day, Patsy Cline is covered head to toe in pink, just like Vera Bogg. She looks like a big mound of cotton candy that is so sweet and sugary, it makes the teeth want to drop right out of my mouth.

"What is that?" I ask Patsy, the first chance I get. Which happens to be on the way to recess right after Miss Stunkel makes us take a surprise test on decimal points.

"What?" she says, like she doesn't even know what she's wearing or how I feel about pink. Then she says, "Oh. These are Vera's. We did an outfit switcheroo."

"Why would you do a thing like that?"

"For fun," she says, playing with the chain on her FRIENDS FOREVER necklace.

"I don't see what's so fun about it."

Patsy Cline says, "Humph," and then nothing else. We stare at each other for a long time after that. This time, I plant my eyeballs on Marge the caterpillar like there's nothing else in the world to look at. I stare so long and so hard that Marge starts to wiggle and squirm.

And just when Marge is about to smile at me and turn into a butterfly, Vera Bogg—wearing Patsy's blue cowgirl shirt!—taps Patsy on the shoulder from behind. Without taking my eyeballs off Patsy, and without blinking, I put on a face that says, Vera Bogg, You're In for a Very Long Wait. But then Patsy does something she's never done before: She stops staring.

"What are you doing?" I say. "What about our staring contest?"

She shrugs. "You win, I guess."

Vera tugs on Patsy's arm. "Let's see who can jump off the swings the farthest."

"Patsy Cline Roberta Watson," I say, grabbing her other arm. "I *never* win."

Patsy pulls free from me and yanks at a strand of hair that's caught in her necklace. "Okay," she says to Vera and then asks me if I want to come swinging. But I can only shake my head, because Patsy's been brainwashed.

After recess, all *my* brains can think about is what is happening to Patsy Cline. Even though her desk is in the next row, she seems miles away. Like she's in Alaska. Because Vera Bogg kidnapped her, wrapped her up in a pink sleeping bag, put her on a pink airplane, and took her there. And I don't know how to get her back.

That's what my brains are thinking about when the last bell rings and Miss Stunkel says in front of everybody, "Penelope Crumb, remember you need to stay after today."

Good gravy. I forgot all about our meeting with Miss Stunkel to talk about me being odd.

Miss Stunkel strokes her Wednesday lizard pin and puts a smile on her face that says You Didn't Think I'd Forget, Did You?

While Patsy Cline and Vera Bogg pack up their book bags to go home, they whisper and nod and give each other the kind of looks that best friends do. The kind that Patsy and me used to do.

After everybody leaves and it's just me and Miss Stunkel left alone together, I keep my head real close to my drawing pad and put on a face that says, Do Not Disturb: Very Serious Business in Progress, so Miss Stunkel won't try to talk to me.

But it doesn't work, because Miss Stunkel tells me to make myself useful and go outside and bang the chalk dust out of the erasers while we wait for my mom. I take a long time doing this and don't go back inside until I see my mom in the hallway.

I wait outside the door to Miss Stunkel's classroom and am real quiet just in case Mom and Miss

Stunkel decide they are going to talk about me. But all I can hear is Miss Stunkel saying something nice about my mom's shirt and then my mom says something I can't hear and then Miss Stunkel laughs.

That's when I know I'm in trouble. Because Miss Stunkel does not laugh ever. I mean, never ever. Didn't know she could, even. "People sure aren't acting like themselves today," I whisper to Leonardo, "and I don't like it."

Meanwhile, the chalk dust from banging erasers must have drifted into my nose because even though I'm trying to be quiet, my nose has an awful tickle, and I let out a really loud sneeze. The erasers fall to the floor. Miss Stunkel says, "Penelope? Is that you?" I sneeze again and tell her that I'll be right there.

But as I bend down to pick up the erasers, something shiny in the corner by the coatrack gets my attention: a white sand dollar necklace, the chain piled in a clump. I scoop it up and examine it in the palm of my hand. The chain has some hair threaded through it, the color of cherry chocolate fudge. And right away I know whose necklace this is. I squeeze it tight in my palm and slip it into my pocket.

"There you are," says Mom at the door. "Come on in so we don't waste Miss Stunkel's time."

I return the erasers to the chalkboard, and Miss Stunkel tells me to pull up a chair next to her desk beside my mom. Then Miss Stunkel starts talking and talking, every once in a while looking at me with a face that says, Penelope Really Is a Bushel of Moldy Peaches. But that's okay because I give her a look right back that says, Whatever You Say, Miss Stunkel. Even though I'm really not listening to most anything she says.

Every once in a while I hear her say the words *concerned* and *unruly* and *behavior problem*. And *odd*. And then *special* and *report* and *why museums are important*.

But my brains aren't bothered with those words

so much. Instead they are on the necklace in my pocket. I rub my finger over the words FRIENDS FOREVER. If anybody is going to be friends forever, it should be me and Patsy. It's not that I don't like Vera Bogg or anything, except for maybe all that pink. It's just that when you start to lose someone, like your best friend, for example, you have to do something.

10.

In the car on the way home, Mom pushes the buttons on the radio and asks me what I think.

"About what?" I say.

She finds a station playing music that's got no words. The fast kind that's busy with a lot of instruments and noise and makes my head hurt. "About what Miss Stunkel said in there. What we talked about."

"Oh, that," I say. "Fine. No problem."

"Really?" says Mom, tapping her fingers on the steering wheel. "Just like that?"

"Yep," I say. "Just like that."

"Okay, then," says Mom, smiling. "Great."

Which makes me think that I should not listen to Miss Stunkel more often, because then everybody is happy.

At home, I lay Patsy's necklace on a plate and slide it into the middle of the closet. Then I make a card about the necklace that says

> Sand dollar necklace belonging
> to Patsy Cline Roberta Watson, best
> friend of Penelope Crumb (except
> maybe not right now), found in hallway
> of Portwaller Elementary School.

And one for the hair:

> Frizzed-out hair from Patsy Cline
> Roberta Watson, best friend of
> Penelope Crumb (used to be, and I hope
> will be again soon), found in the chain
> of sand dollar necklace.

Before closing the door, I take one more look at

the shoehorn and Patsy Cline's necklace and hair and decide they could use some company. A dark, mostly empty closet can be kind of scary, after all. Patsy Cline is allergic to things with tails, but I'm not so sure about her necklace and hair. I, Penelope Crumb, don't believe in closet monsters anymore, especially those with tails, but you can never be too sure, I guess.

I scan my bookshelf. Behind my *Max Adventure* action figures, baby-doll heads (Terrible won't tell me what he did with the rest of them), pet rock collection, and Mistletoe Mouse Woodland Family play set, is a heart-shaped tin that my aunt Renn bought me for my last birthday. I shimmy off the lid and count the number of teeth in my collection: five.

I started collecting my teeth a couple of years ago after the Tooth Fairy forgot to take one from under my pillow. (She left me a dollar anyway, thank lucky stars.) Not too long ago, I got the idea to put the same old tooth under my pillow a couple days in a row just to see what would happen. I didn't get any more money, and that's when Terrible told me, "Mom is the Tooth Fairy, stupid." But I'm not sure I believe him, because if there's one thing I've learned, it's that aliens can't be trusted.

Littie gets all grossed out when I show her my teeth collection, especially the ones with blood on them. But you never know when you might need old teeth. Like now, for example.

I set the tin beside the dinner plate. "This will keep away any closet monsters." Then I curl up in the corner of the museum and close my eyes. Patsy Cline would be so happy to know that I'm taking good care of her necklace. Not that I'm going to tell her or anything.

11.

Miss Stunkel calls me over to her desk before the first bell. I don't know how I could be in any trouble when all I've done so far is sit at my desk and wait for Patsy Cline. But it doesn't take much to get into trouble with Miss Stunkel.

"Penelope," Miss Stunkel says in a low voice, "I wanted to tell you that I like how agreeable you were last evening during our talk."

I stare at the wrinkles in her forehead while I wait for the bad part. Miss Stunkel scrunches her eyebrows, which makes even more forehead wrinkles, but the part where she says I'm a disappointment doesn't come. Then she nods at me real slow, like it's my turn to talk.

Only, I don't know what I'm supposed to say. So I just nod real slow right back and say, "I like how agreeable you were last evening, too."

Miss Stunkel lets out a "wah" that sort of sounds like a laugh, but not really. Then my big nose, which has superpowers, catches a whiff of her breath. And it smells like potato salad, heavy on the mayonnaise. "I'll be eager to see your report on Monday."

"My report?" I say.

"Yes, your report, Penelope. The one we talked about last evening." Then she sticks out her jaw at me like she thinks I'm playing around. Which I very am not doing. "The one about museums? Why they are important? You do remember talking about this, don't you?" Her finger starts to come out of her pocket.

I nod my head and put a look on my face that

says, Oh, That Report. Yes, Indeedy, I Remember That One. Which must work, because Miss Stunkel's finger goes back inside her pocket.

She says, "All right. You can go back to your seat now."

Good gravy.

Patsy Cline is at her desk when Miss Stunkel is done with me, and on my way to her, I spot Vera Bogg across the room. She's about as far away from Patsy as I am, and she's heading for her, too. I get my legs going, but somehow Vera's legs are faster. She gets to Patsy's desk before me. By the time I make it there, Patsy and Vera are already talking.

I squeeze myself between them and the first thing that comes out of my mouth is, "Miss Stunkel eats potato salad for breakfast."

Nobody knows what to say next, including me. But then to my surprise, after a while, Vera Bogg says, "I like potato salad with hard-boiled eggs." And also to my surprise, the whole time Patsy is giving me a look that says, Did You Eat Glue Again?

I don't answer her. But I do notice that Vera Bogg is wearing her sand dollar necklace and Patsy isn't. Vera notices that, too, because then she says, "Patsy, where's your necklace?"

I wait for Patsy to say that she lost her necklace, that it's nowhere to be found, and that it doesn't matter anyway because it was a dumb idea to get matching necklaces with you, Vera Bogg, if you want to know the truth. But Patsy doesn't say those things. Instead, she looks down where her necklace would be (if it wasn't in my museum closet next to my teeth) and tells Vera that she took it off this morning so that it wouldn't get messed up while she ate her breakfast and then she forgot to put it on.

"What?" I say.

Patsy repeats the part about the breakfast and then starts chewing on her eraser.

My word. Patsy Cline Roberta Watson *never* tells lies. And she's really bad at it.

But Vera must not think so, because she just

smiles and says, "Oh, that's okay. We can be matching tomorrow."

Patsy's face looks like she's in pain, like maybe telling that big lie hurts inside. She looks so awful that it almost makes me want to give her necklace back. But then the thought of Patsy and Vera being the kind of friends that switch outfits and buy matching stuff makes me hurt inside, too, so I keep quiet.

"Don't forget again, okay?" says Vera before going to her desk.

"Okay," says Patsy Cline softly.

I give Patsy a look that says, That Was a Real Whopper.

But Patsy isn't as good as me at telling what different kinds of faces mean, so when she catches me staring, she says, "What, Penelope?" And her words are spears.

"Nothing," I say back, all pretendy that I don't know what is going on and am waiting for her to tell *me*, Penelope Crumb, her supposed-to-be best friend, the truth. But she doesn't. "Want to come over after school?"

She shakes her head. "No, thanks."

"Why not?"

"I have some things needing tending," she says.

"Like what kind of things?"

"Just things." Then she pulls her math book out of her desk and opens it.

"Patsy Cline, if you don't want to tell me what things, then just say so."

She stares at me all serious-like and gives me a look that says she doesn't.

"Humph," I say and then nothing else. If Patsy Cline doesn't know she's supposed to talk to me about her problems, then I'm not going to be the one to tell her.

12.

I have to do a report for Miss Stunkel?" I say to Mom as soon as she gets home.

"Nice to see you, too, Penelope," she says. "Do you mind if I take my coat off and put my bag down?"

I help pull off her coat and slide the bag off of her shoulder. The bag is loaded full of books, probably on brains, and it drops to the floor. "Careful," she says.

"How come you didn't tell me?" This is what I want to know.

Mom says, "Penelope Rae." (Swollen abdomen.)

"What?"

"You were sitting right there when Miss Stunkel told us all about it," she says.

"Well, why do I have to do it?"

Mom says, "Because Miss Stunkel is under the impression that you don't think museums are worth good behavior."

"Why does she think that?"

"Oh, I don't know. Maybe from your outburst and disrupting the whole experience for your class."

I don't see how my outbursting could be disrupting when all everybody was doing was just shopping, anyway. But I decide to keep this to myself. "I do like museums," I say. "I like them a whole lot." For a second or two, I think about telling her about the museum in my closet. So she'll know that I'm not pretending. But my museum isn't the kind that's open to visitors.

"Then you shouldn't have any problem showing how much you like them in your report."

"Fine," I say. But it really isn't.

My museum floor is getting a little crowded, so I curl up in a corner, hugging my knees to my chest. I look over what I have so far: a necklace, hair, some teeth, and a shoehorn. Only, the teeth don't count because they are just there for protection.

"A museum is not truly a museum without some art," I can practically hear Leonardo say. And he would be right.

After Mom goes to bed, I sneak into the laundry room. I switch on the light, and this time it's me surprising Terrible. Apparently you can sneak up on an alien, because he jumps and yells, and he must have had some of Mom's drawing pencils in his hand, because they spill everywhere.

"What are you doing with Mom's good pencils?" I say. "They're supposed to be just for drawing."

On his hands and knees, he reaches underneath the dryer/desk to get the pencils that rolled away. "So?"

"So, you don't draw," I say. "You don't even like art."

He gets to his feet and shoves the pencils back into the glass jars on the dryer/desk. Then he starts to walk away, but I plant my feet wide apart and block him. I get a look on my face that says, I'm Not Afraid of You. Even though I kind of am. Aliens are like dogs, though, and he must sense the fear in me, because he shows me his alien teeth and lets out a growl.

"Move," he says.

And I do, but not because he said so. Because I am on official museum business.

After he's long gone, I look around the laundry room to see if I can tell what Terrible is really up to. But all I see are brains. Drawings of them, I mean. All different sizes, and all full of wrinkles. There are piles of books of people's insides on the desk/dryer. And a stack of drawing pads on Mom's wooden stool.

I pick up a drawing pad from the top of the

stack and start flipping through it. Lots of creepy insides—brains, hearts, and one that looks like a giant, puffed-up worm that says "lower intestine." More of the same in the next two. When I get to the one on the bottom of the pile, I'm expecting to see more creepy insides, but instead on each page is a drawing of my mom.

I knew Mom was just as good at drawing people's outsides as she is at drawing their insides, but she doesn't do it very much, so I forget. It isn't easy to draw yourself, that I know. I can only draw my face if I trace around it, and even then, with my big nose, I end up looking more like a penguin with long hair than me, a non-penguin-type person.

My mom doesn't have a big, stand-out nose like me and Grandpa Felix. Her nose is thin and small and suits her face just fine. The most stand-out part of her is her eyes. They are big and round and blue, and when she's happy, you just want to dive right into them and do the backstroke.

In these drawings, though, Mom's eyes are shut. There are no big pools of blue to go swimming in. I don't know why she would draw herself that way, because truth be told, without her eyes, she doesn't even look like Mom. I keep turning the pages, hoping that she'll open her eyes and see me and invite me in.

But she never does. That's when I decide that maybe what Mom needs is some help in the eyeball department. I take her drawings back to my room, and on every page, I erase her shut eyes and draw wide open ones that say, Come On In—the Water's Fine.

"Oh me, oh my, this is splendid," Leonardo would say. "Thank lucky stars that she has you around to help."

Then I grab another plate from the kitchen cupboard and set the drawing pad on it, open to the first page. The card I make says this:

Drawings of Mom Crumb by Mom
Crumb, who is an excellent insides and

outsides artist. Eyeballs by Penelope
Crumb.

This is becoming a real museum, I say to myself. Now I won't ever forget.

13.

What do you think of this one?" asks Grandpa Felix, sliding a photograph to me across his kitchen table.

He got the pictures made from the wedding, and he's checking over his work before handing them in. In this picture, the bride and groom are standing under an archway holding hands.

"Good," I say.

"What's good about it?"

I study the picture. "Well, for one thing, they are both smiling."

"That's the best you can do?" He raps his finger on the picture.

"Okay." I try again. "They don't have red eyes or anything. And you didn't get your thumb in the way, which is what usually happens when Mom takes pictures." I slide the photograph back to him. "Like I said, good."

Grandpa Felix shakes his head. Then he grumbles something about wedding photography and puts that picture in a pile with others.

"Don't you like weddings?"

"Not particularly."

"Me neither," I say. "I mean, I've only been to one, Aunt Renn's. But Mom made me wear pantyhose and shoes that pinched my feet, and after it was over, they ran out of yellow cheese before I could get any."

"Sounds hideous." Then he pauses and says, "That means really terrible and awful."

"It was," I say. "Hideous. But taking pictures at weddings isn't so bad."

Grandpa Felix scratches his whiskers and says,

"If you say so." He slides his chair back from the table. "You can never go back."

I'm not sure where he wants to go back to, but before I have a chance to ask, he says, "Coffee?" Then he smiles at me, and the creases in his face get deeper.

"Grandpa Felix."

"Oh, right, I forgot. You're trying to cut back. Wise girl."

As he takes a mug from the cupboard, I weave through the piles of pictures stacked knee-high on the floor. There are so many that, no matter how many times I visit, I always find new ones. Well, ones that are new to me, I mean. This time I find one of a hummingbird, so close up, you can see green feathers on its belly.

"Botanical gardens, on assignment for *Life*," he says when I show him the picture. "I had to hold still for more than an hour to snap that one. I can remember I was suffering from allergies awful that day, so it took a lot out of me not to sneeze."

That hummingbird's got a surprised look on

his face like he is supposed to be on a diet but got caught with two scoops of butter pecan ice cream. I tell Grandpa Felix this, and it makes him laugh. "Butter pecan?"

I look at the hummingbird again and nod. "It's his favorite."

Grandpa shakes his head at me and smiles. "Ah, Penelope."

Getting Grandpa Felix to smile isn't easy, but it's something I like to try to do. Because when he smiles, sometimes I can see my dad in his face. "When I found out that you weren't Graveyard Dead, I thought you might be a world adventurer, catching rare butterflies or something."

"Is that so?" he says. I tell him that it is so, and he says sorry to disappoint.

"You didn't disappoint," I say. "You were out on adventures catching hummingbirds, except with a camera instead of a net."

His face begins to fall a little. So I dive into another pile to find something that might prop it back up again. A black-and-white picture of a gigantic waterfall looks like it might do the trick. I pull it from the pile, but when I do, a piece of paper the size of a postcard floats to the floor.

> *Mr. Crumb,*
>
> *Thank you for your application for the position of staff photographer with* Living in Portwaller *magazine. We received applications from many people. After reviewing your submitted application materials, we have decided that we will not offer you an interview.*
>
> *Best of luck in your pursuits.*

"What's this?" I say, bringing the card to him.

He sets his cup of coffee down on the table and squints at the card. Then he takes it from me and tosses it into the trash. "That's nothing. Which is just about what my life as a photographer is worth these days. Forty years working for the big boys, and now I can't even get a job taking pictures for a small-time rag."

"I didn't know you wanted to get a job with that magazine," I say.

"I don't." He pats me on the head. "I don't."

"But then why—"

"You can't go back," he says. "Once it's gone, it's gone." He sighs and then looks at the piles of pictures about the room. "Sometimes you just have to let go."

"You can't let go," I say. Especially when I've been trying so hard to hold on.

"It's just as well." He picks up a picture from the top of a pile. "It's about time I did something with all of these. Good timing, too. My landlord is having all the apartments painted, so I've got to get this stuff out of here."

"What are you going to do?"

"Right now, I'm going to lie down." His shoulders are in such a slump when he walks away that I'm afraid he might break in half. He doesn't, somehow, but after he closes the door to his bedroom, it's just me with all of his things.

"You shouldn't let go," I say quietly. And then to the piles. "I'm not letting go."

I can almost hear Grandpa Felix's cameras, his friends, in their bags over by the bookcase, clicking away in agreement. From the small brown leather bag, I pull out Alfred, keeping a listen for Grandpa. Alfred is solid and cold in my cupped hands. The silver buttons and knobs are pebble-smooth and have what's left of a shine that's been rubbed dull by Grandpa's big rough hands.

"Alfred," I whisper, placing it carefully in my toolbox next to my drawing pad, "you are coming with me."

14.

As the metro rattles and shakes, I hold tight to my toolbox. At every stop, I peek inside, just a peek, to make sure Alfred isn't getting jarred around too much. And maybe, every once in a while, just maybe, I might even say something like "You okay in there?" and "Wait until you see your new home," until a woman in the seat behind me taps me on the shoulder and says, "What you got in there? A kitten?"

No, I tell her, just a camera. She scrunches up her forehead like she doesn't believe me and says,

"Come on, now." So I let her see real quick. But I think she must have been really hoping to see a kitten in there, because afterward she gives me a mean look that says, Don't You Try to Make a Fool of Me. And then she moves to another seat.

After that, I keep my toolbox shut for the rest of the way home.

When I get to our apartment building, Littie and her momma are on the way out. Momma Maple says hello to me, but Littie gives me a fake smile that says, I Still Want to Know What's in Your Closet.

I give her a look that says, I Don't Know What You're Talking About, and then I go inside.

I borrow another plate from our cupboard and put Alfred on it, right next to Patsy Cline's necklace and hair. Then I make a card that says

Alfred the camera, belongs to Felix Crumb, excellent photographer and grandpa.

. . .

There's some trouble between Patsy and Vera Bogg, thank lucky stars. I know this because on the way to my desk, Patsy Cline grabs my arm and pulls me over to Miss Stunkel's bulletin board. Under the big green letters ORGANIZATION IS THE KEY TO SUCCESS, Patsy whispers to me, "I've got trouble."

"You're wearing a turtleneck shirt," I say. Which she doesn't ever do, because turtles have tails.

She says yes, scratching her elbow, but that's not the problem. Then she looks over my shoulder and says, "I need to tell you something."

I can't help but smile. Finally, Patsy Cline is going to tell me her problem just like a best friend should.

"You remember the shell necklace that I got at the Portwaller History Museum?"

"I'm not sure," I say, because when you're pretending not to know something, you have to act like you don't have it sitting on a dinner plate in your closet at home.

"It says 'friends forever.' The same as Vera's. You don't remember?"

"I don't know," I say. "Is it a necklace?"

"I just said it was a necklace," says Patsy. "Anyway, I lost it somehow."

I say, "You did? Where? In here? In the hallway by the coatrack?" Pretending is harder than it looks.

"Penelope, if I knew where I lost it, then it wouldn't be lost," she says. "It would be found. And I would be wearing it right now. What's the matter with you?"

"Oh, right. Sorry."

"The trouble is, Vera keeps asking about it, but I don't know what to tell her."

"Just tell her you lost it," I say. "Or wait! Let *me* tell her for you."

"No," Patsy says. "Vera is different."

"She's different, all right," I say, shaking my head. "All that pink."

Patsy Cline rolls her eyeballs at me and says that's not what she means. And then she says in a shy voice, "I want her to like me."

"Why?"

She huffs. "So she'll be my friend."

Those words practically kill me dead. I'm left behind again, just like in the Portwaller History Museum, alone with all the other things that have been left behind. This is what it feels like to be a mangy teddy. "What about me?" I ask, holding my breath. Before she has a chance to answer, Vera Bogg is beside us.

"Do you think we'll have a surprise quiz today on percentages?" Vera asks, staring at Patsy.

Patsy looks like she's having some sort of allergy attack from her shirt and doesn't answer. So I say, "I think we have a fifty percent chance." Which is a pretty clever thing to say, in my opinion. But Vera just looks at me all serious and says, "Really?"

Well, then.

Vera goes on about how Miss Stunkel likes to give surprise quizzes, which everybody already knows anyway. And the whole time Vera's talking, she's got ahold of her necklace, sliding the sand dollar back and forth along the chain and staring at Patsy's turtled neck. Finally, she says, "Did you forget your necklace again, Patsy Cline?"

Now Patsy looks like she's the one that's going to die. "Ummm, well, ummm. I don't know. Ummm, lost."

"Lost?" says Vera. "Where?"

"If she knew where she lost it," I say, "then it wouldn't be lost. It would be found. And then it would be hanging around her neck." Then I give Patsy a look that says, Aren't You Lucky to Have Me for a Best Friend?

But Patsy must not think she's very lucky at all, because she says, "Don't be that way, Penelope." And then she says to Vera, "The chain kept getting caught in my hair. And I took it off for a minute and then it got lost. I'm sorry we can't be matching anymore."

I don't know what Patsy expected Vera Bogg to do, but all she says is, "I can help you look for it."

All at once Patsy seems to be over her allergic reaction. And she has a smile on her face like I haven't seen. And somehow, even without matching necklaces, Patsy is still on her way to being gone.

15.

Sitting cross-legged in my Ultra Museum of Forget-Me-Notters, I hold Patsy Cline's sand dollar necklace in my palm and wonder when Patsy will forget about me. I've been trying so hard to make sure I won't forget about everybody else, but how can I make sure I won't be forgotten?

Then I think that maybe what Patsy needs is a necklace to remember me by. To remember that I'm her best friend, to remember so that she won't want to be gone anymore.

I choose one of my best teeth from the tin box,

and then I grab one hair from the top of my head and yank. Which hurts a lot, so I only do one more. I wrap the two hairs around my tooth and tie the whole thing together with a thin red ribbon I find in my arts and crafts drawer. Then I cut out a big *P* and a *C* from a piece of paper in my drawing pad.

All the paper, glue, and glitter anyone could ever want is in with my arts and crafts supplies, but no string. I search the kitchen drawers and cupboards, but I only come up with a rubber band and a twist tie from a loaf of bread.

On the way back to my room, I stop at Terrible's door and lean my ear against the stickers that read KEEP OUT! and DANGER! and IF YOU CAN READ THIS, YOU ARE TOO CLOSE! I knock softly and then push open the door. "Are you in here?" I squint into the dark room, but I don't see or smell him.

I feel along the wall for the light switch and flick it on. Unlike my room, Terrible's room is neat and organized. You can even see the floor. Because here's something I know about aliens: They don't like messes. No dirty clothes on the floor, no half-eaten sandwiches on the desk, no dust even. And too bad for me—not one piece of string anywhere.

While I'm looking, though, I find a stack of spiral notebooks in his top desk drawer. Good gravy, alien diaries. I pull one out and open it. NASA might like to know how an alien thinks. But instead of any "Dear Diary, Today I found two kittens in the sewer and ate them for breakfast" (because that's what aliens do), there's a beautiful drawing of a building. It's got more than twenty levels, and windows in the shape of triangles.

At first I think this might be a building from Terrible's home planet, but then at the bottom of the building, he drew cars and a stoplight. And everybody knows that aliens don't drive, so . . . On the next page, another building. This one is a house with a big garden in the back and a front yard with flowers and green grass. He even drew what each room in the house looks like and labeled them. The regular stuff like a kitchen and bathrooms and bedrooms. But he also drew a proper office for Mom, with a real desk, a big room marked "Terrence" that has its own bathroom, and then . . .

"Oh me, oh my," I say. There's a room with my name on it that says "Penelope's Art Room." Oh, wouldn't I love to live in a place like this with my own artist's room! Imagine the size of a museum that I could fit in there! I tuck the notebook under my arm, because this is the Terrible I'd like to remember.

I make a card for my museum that says

Drawings by Terrible Crumb, pain-in-the-neck space alien, secret artist, and sometimes pretty nice brother to Penelope Crumb.

I can practically hear Leonardo say, "An artistic mind brings a brother and sister closer than they think."

"He's still an alien," I say back. "And I still need a string for Patsy's necklace." I gently roll

Drawings by
Terrible Crumb,
pain-in-the-ne[c]
secret-artist, a[
pretty nice bro
Penelope Cru

the tooth-wrapped hair between my thumb and pointer until I come up with the best idea ever: dental floss, peppermint-flavored and waxed. Which I think will work out fine, because when Patsy wears this necklace, she will also be able to get raisins out of her teeth.

While I'm stringing up Patsy's necklace with floss, there's a racket coming from the laundry room, loud enough that I can hear it in my closet. The shuffling of papers and smacking of books. Then Mom's voice. "Where in the world did I put that?"

I keep on stringing. "Patsy Cline won't soon forget about me once I give her this necklace," I whisper to Leonardo. "Indeed, you are an original forget-me-notter," he would surely say. Which makes me smile.

"Has anybody seen my blue sketch pad?" Mom's voice again.

I freeze and stare at the blue sketch pad in front of me. Then, real quick, I close the door to my closet and hide.

16.

I wait for Patsy Cline by the coatrack outside
of Miss Stunkel's classroom, holding on tight
to her necklace. The smell of the peppermint
makes me want to floss something, so I hope Patsy
gets here soon.

My heart jumps in my throat when I see Patsy,
and then stops beating when I see that Vera Bogg
beside her. As they get closer, I can tell that they've
switched outfits again—Patsy is in a pink shirt
with ruffles down the front. And that's when I
know that Patsy, this new Patsy in her pink Vera

Bogg ruffles and big smile, would never wear the necklace I made for her. This Patsy Cline would only wear store-bought.

I shove the necklace under my arm so they won't see. Then I try one last thing.

"I found it," I say. "I found your necklace."

"You did?" says Patsy, giving me a big smile— a smile like she was just given a pony made out of marshmallows. "Honest to goodness?"

"True blue," I say.

"Where?" asks Vera Bogg.

"Right here by the coatrack."

"No, I mean where is it?"

"Oh," I say. "It's at home." Then I tell a partly true story about how I found the necklace (which is true) yesterday (which is not) after everybody left, and took it home to keep it safe (sort of true) but forgot to bring it with me today (not). "I'll bring it Monday."

Patsy Cline hugs me just then and whispers "Thank you" in my ear. I hug her, too, and it feels like we might be back to being best friends again. And maybe if I just hold on tight to her, I can break Vera Bogg's spell and Patsy won't be gone from me again. But while I'm holding on to her, I forget about the necklace stuffed under my arm, and it falls to the floor.

Of course Vera Bogg would notice. "What's that?" she says.

Patsy lets go of me.

"What?" I say.

"That," she says, bending down to pick it up.

"Oh *that*," I say. "*That* is a necklace."

Then that Vera Bogg brings it closer to her face like she hasn't ever seen a necklace before in her life. "What's it for?"

"It was *for* Patsy Cline," I say, folding my arms across my chest. Patsy's eyes get big, and she has a look on her face that says, Really, for Me? And I'm about to say, "Yes, for you, Patsy Cline," but Vera Bogg's scream gets in the way.

"A tooth!" shouts Vera Bogg. "A tooth!" She

drops the necklace, and me and Patsy Cline bend down at the same time to get it. Patsy gets there first. She scoops it up.

The screams are still coming out of Vera's mouth, murdering screams, and her mouth is open so wide when she's hollering that I can practically see her tonsils. Which are also pink. And she doesn't stop until Miss Stunkel comes running. "Mercy! What is happening out here?"

Vera Bogg points to the necklace in Patsy's hands and yells, "A tooth!" for the hundredth time.

Miss Stunkel says, "Let me see, Patsy." And then she takes the necklace from Patsy, holding it up by the floss. Meanwhile, other kids from my class, including Angus Meeker, are crowding around trying to see who's being killed. "There's a *P* and a *C*," says Miss Stunkel. "And, yes, Vera, that appears to be a tooth." Then she points her chicken-bone finger at me and bends the tip toward her. "Penelope Crumb, follow me."

I follow her all the way to her desk. "Is this yours?" she says.

"The necklace or the tooth?"

"This," she says, holding it away from her, "is a necklace?"

I nod. "It's not mine, really, because I made it for Patsy Cline. It belongs to her. We have the same initials."

"And the tooth is . . . ?"

"Mine."

She sighs. "Yours." Then she hands me the necklace and tells me to see her after school because I've given her no choice but to send a note home about this one.

Good gravy.

"Here," I say, handing Mom the note from Miss Stunkel as soon as I get home.

"Penelope," she says. "Not again."

I save her from the pain of having to read it and tell her what happened. "I brought a tooth to school for Patsy Cline."

"What kind of tooth?"

"The kind that came from my mouth."

She says, "Don't be smart." Which I really wasn't being.

"Not one with blood on it," I say.

"Penelope Rae." (Dislocated knee.) She stuffs the note inside her purse. "We'll talk about this later. I've got to go see Felix. He had some people in his apartment to paint, and he thinks they took some things."

My cheeks start to burn. "Took some things?"

Mom grabs her keys from the hall table and then shakes her head. "I don't know how he can tell anything's missing, with the way he keeps that place."

"Something's missing? What's he missing?" Then I cup my hands over my ears because I'm afraid what she's going to say. But somehow her voice still gets through my fingers because I can still hear Mom say, "Probably nothing. You know Felix." And just when I think it's safe to take my hands away from my ears, she says, "I'm not sure—something about a camera."

That's when I practically go dead.

Mom doesn't seem to notice, though, because she is halfway out the door when she turns and says, "Anyway, your brother is in charge. Which reminds me. Terrence!" she hollers.

He yells back from his room. "What?"

"It's your turn to do dishes. And please be more careful with our dinner plates. They aren't expensive, but we're down to two now, and if you keep breaking them, we'll be eating right off the table."

Terrible sticks his head out of his door. "I didn't break any dishes. Ask *her*." He means me. And the way he says it, I wonder if he knows about my museum. If he knows it was me that took the plates. And the other things, too.

I get sweaty nervous all of a sudden. I shake my head at my mom and say, "Wasn't me." And then I don't know what makes me do this next thing, because I could have just stopped right then and there, but I guess I'm scared of having my museum discovered and also about taking Alfred, so I jab my thumb down the hall toward Terrible's room and whisper, "He probably didn't do it on purpose. You know, he is kind of clumsy."

Mom winks at me and smiles, like she knows that Terrible can't help breaking things. Then she asks me if I feel okay because I'm looking kind of pale in the face, and I tell her that I think I need to go lie down.

She touches the end of my nose with her finger and says, "Good idea. And tell Littie she can stay for supper if she wants, if it's okay with her momma."

"Huh?" is the only thing I can say, because when you're practically dead, it's hard to talk much.

"Littie's over," Mom says before leaving. "She's in your room."

The thought of Littie in my room BY HER-SELF gets me alive again, so I race down the hall and shove open the door. "Littie Maple!"

She doesn't answer right away. And then a small bird voice squeaks from inside my closet. "I'm. In. Here." Before I can say anything else, she appears in the doorway with her fists on her hips and a look on her face that says, You've Got Trouble.

"You're not supposed to be in there," I tell her. No one is supposed to know about my museum, or about the things I took.

She shakes her head at me, and I wait for her to say how I am going to be in big trouble if anybody finds out what I've done. But then I see a silver chain peeking out from her closed fist.

17.

"hat are you doing with that?" I say.

Littie opens her hand and says, "What are YOU doing with it?"

"Nothing." And then I remember what I told Patsy. "I'm giving it back. To Patsy Cline."

"You made a museum," she says.

I nod and then hold out my hand for the necklace. But Littie puts her hand behind her back.

"You could have told me what you were up to," she says. "I'm just saying."

"I didn't want anybody to know. You aren't

going to tell, are you, Littie?" I wiggle my eyebrows at her so she knows I mean business.

Littie puckers her lip like she's not so sure. "Why do you call it the Ultra Museum of Forget-Me-Notters?"

"So that I won't forget about people. And because they are important enough to be in a museum."

Littie's face turns bright red at that. "Well, that's really a fly in a bowl of corn chowder, isn't it? I guess I'm not important enough to be in your museum. Just like I wasn't important enough to know about the museum in the first place. If we're not friends anymore, then just say so."

"Littie . . ."

"I mean I know I'm homeschooled and everything, and I may not have as many friends as you, and sometimes I am a little bit too nosy, I know, but—"

"Littie—"

"That doesn't mean you should leave me behind . . ."

My word. I tell Littie that we are friends, and she says, "Friends forever?"

"Yes, Littie."

"Whew!" She puts her hand to her forehead and falls into the Heap.

"And you can be in my museum, too," I say. "If you want."

"I want," she says. "But do you have to keep your teeth in there?" Then she holds out Patsy's necklace to me. I wrap my fingers around the sand dollar and pull, but Littie doesn't let go right away, like she wants me to pull her up out of the Heap. I keep pulling on the necklace, because I'm not letting go of it, and then there's a loud snap under our fingers.

Littie starts to shake all over when she sees what happened. I stare at the part of the sand dollar I'm holding. It says ENDS EVER. And I think that this is the *end* of me and Patsy Cline *ever* being best friends.

"I'm sorry. I'm sorry. I'm sorry. I'm sorry." Littie brings her FRI FOR part to match up with mine, but when we try to fit them back together, the pieces of the sand dollar break even more. Until all that's left is a little pile of sand.

This time I know I will die, and I fall into the Heap, burying my head under my hang-up clothes. I don't know how long I'm dead for, but Littie shakes me alive and says, "How are we going to fix this?"

That's the thing about Littie: She never gives up. There's a fix for everything, that's how her brain works. "I guess glue is out of the question," she says, letting the bits of sand fall through her fingers.

I give her a look that says, I Don't Think This Can Be Fixed.

She says, "All we need is a little brainpower. Let's think."

I squeeze my eyes shut and try to think, but all I can think of is Patsy Cline's face when she sees what's left of her necklace.

"If only we knew where she got it," says Littie.

"I know where. The Portwaller History Museum. What difference does that make?"

Littie rolls her eyeballs at me. "Well, why didn't you say so before? All we have to do is go to the museum and buy a new one."

"That necklace costs money. Fifteen dollars, I think. Do you have fifteen dollars? Because I don't. I left all of my money . . ."

"What?"

I pull myself up from the Heap and grab Littie's hand. "Come on, let's go."

"Where?" she says, her eyes bright.

"Littie Maple, we're going on another adventure."

18.

I tell Littie I'll meet her in front of our building. Then I grab my toolbox and metro card and tip-toe down the hall to Terrible's room. His door is closed, like always, and his music is turned way up, but since he's in charge, I do what I'm supposed to and ask him if it's okay if I go to the museum with Littie. I do this from the hallway in the quietest whisper there is, with my hand over my mouth. If he doesn't know he can't hear what I said, then I'm not going to be the one to tell him.

Littie is waiting for me by the telephone pole,

sliding a moldy hamburger bun with her foot over to a hungry pigeon.

"Where did you get that?" I say.

She points toward our building. "I found it over there by the trash can."

"What did you tell your momma?"

"The truth," she says, flashing the alarm around her neck. "What did you tell your mom?"

"I didn't. She's at my grandpa Felix's helping him look for something." I wince as those words spill out of my mouth. "Something that isn't there."

"What isn't there?" she asks.

"Alfred." I shake my head to try to get that thought out of my brains. "Never mind. Let's just get a new necklace for Patsy Cline."

The metro is crowded, so Littie and I find a place to stand near the back of the train. I set my toolbox by my feet and hold on to the metal pole. A boy with long hair pulled away from his face by a pair of knitted headphones grabs on to the pole above my hand. He reminds me of Terrible, except for the long hair and headphones and the fact that this boy doesn't smell like fishing worms mixed with orange sherbet and furniture polish.

"Littie," I whisper, nudging her with my elbow, "here's a boy that's probably not an alien. Maybe you should like him instead of Terrible."

Littie's eyes get big and she gives me a look that says, I'm Going to Kill You.

And then I say, "If you had an umbrella in your hand, you'd look just like Miss Stunkel."

Littie pretends she doesn't know me after that. The train lurches to a stop at the Seventh Street station, and the boy gets off. Once he's gone, I swing around the pole, holding on with both hands, and knock against Littie until she stops pretending. It works after a while, because finally she turns to me like she knows me and says, "The next stop is us."

I pick up my toolbox, and we head out of the metro station and up the long escalator toward the signs that say PORTWALLER HISTORY MUSEUM.

"You never did say how you are going to buy

another necklace without any money," she says as we climb the brick steps of the museum.

"I have money." I pull open the door and lead the way to the donation box. "Here," I say, pointing to the box. "I put in fifteen dollars and fourteen cents plus a Canadian penny during our field trip with Miss Stunkel." I stick two fingers through the slot in the top of the box and feel around.

"What are you doing?" Littie yells, pulling on my arm. "You can't take your money back."

I shove my fingers in deeper. "I don't need all of it back. They can have the fourteen cents and the Canadian penny."

"But it belongs to the museum now!"

"I'll put it back whenever I get some more money," I tell her. "How else am I going to get a new necklace for Patsy Cline?"

Littie keeps pulling my fingers out of the box while I keep trying to stick them in. Littie has bird fingers, which aren't very strong, thank lucky stars, so she has a hard time prying mine away.

But she tries and tries until one time it's not Littie's hands that stop me. These hands have lots of hair on them, and they're big and rough, like they could juice an apple with just one squeeze.

"What's going on here?" says a man in a gray suit with a red bow tie. He's got a face like a lumberjack, with wooly gray whiskers and a flat nose that wouldn't get in the way of tree climbing.

"Umm," says Littie.

I pull out my fingers from the slot and tell him how I put money in this box the other day to help dead people everywhere, and how now I need to get it back to buy a necklace.

When I'm done talking, he nods and strokes his whiskers, and I give Littie a look that says, It's Going to Be Okay. But she must not think so, because she's backing away from me very slowly toward the door.

"Where are your parents?" says the man.

"My mom is at my grandpa Felix's, looking for a camera that I have in my closet at home," I say. "And my dad is Graveyard Dead."

Then he says, "Come with me." Here's one more person that doesn't like me talking about dead things.

Littie says, "We aren't allowed to go anywhere with strangers."

He points to his name tag. "The name is Jack. I work here at the museum."

"He's a lumberjack," I whisper to Littie.

"Nice to meet you, Jack," she tells him. "But you're still a stranger."

Jack grabs my arm at the elbow. "And you two are thieves. Trying to steal from the donation box."

"We weren't stealing," I say, pulling away from him. "Honest."

"I know what I saw." He points to my toolbox. "I suppose you just bring that with you for no reason."

I don't know what that has to do with the price of baloney, but I say, "It belonged to my Graveyard Dead dad."

"We'll let the police sort it out," he says. And then he grabs my arm again.

"Littie!" I point to the black box around her neck.

"Oh! Good thinking," she says. And then she pulls the alarm. WONK!! WONK!! WONK!! WONK!! WONK!! WONK!! WONK!! WONK!! WONK!! WONK!! WONK!! WONK!! WONK!! WONK!! WONK!! WONK!! WONK!! WONK!!

Over the noise of the alarm, Lumberjack Jack says a word I'm not supposed to hear and then lets go of my arm. That's when I grab Littie's hand and we run out of the museum all the way to the metro station. We take turns looking back to make sure he's not chasing us. And every now and then, I check the trees, too, because that's how lumberjacks travel.

Just outside the metro station, we stop to catch our breath. A man in green sunglasses and a red baseball cap is selling pocketbooks spread out on a table. "We've got the real thing here. Real thing right here. Can't beat these prices. I'll make you a

deal. Which one do you like?" He holds up a purple one with a big gold buckle on the front. "Hey,
girls. You like this one? Come here a minute. How
much you pay?"

Littie wraps her fingers around her alarm, but I
stop her and say, "It's okay, Littie. I know how we
can get money for Patsy's necklace."

19.

I pull out my sketch pad from my toolbox and start tearing off drawings. I line each one up against the concrete wall near the entrance to the metro station. First an egg, a mason jar of Mom's charcoal pencils, a tube of ultramarine paint, the sandal that Littie tried on, Terrible's ENTER AT YOUR OWN RISK sticker, Patsy Cline's hand, and then Grandpa Felix asleep on his couch. And lastly Alfred.

"What are you up to?" says Littie.

"How much do you think I should charge?"

"Two dollars apiece?" she says. "There are eight

drawings here, so if you sold all of them, you'd have enough for the necklace. Of course, it would be a better business model if you could make a profit, so you could charge three dollars each and have some money left over. But what if three dollars is too much, and you don't sell them all?"

I give Littie a look that says, How Do You Know All of This Stuff?

"Just say two dollars or best offer," she says.

I say okay and then watch the people that go by. Some don't even look at the drawings, like they aren't even there, and others give them sideways looks and then keep going. Which is almost worse.

"You have to get out there and talk to people," Littie says. "You can't wait for them to come to you. That's what Morgan Trunk always says." Then she steps into a crowd of people about to go onto the escalator and says, "Watch me, Penelope."

"Sir," Littie says to some man with a briefcase, "you failed to notice several lovely drawings by an up-and-coming artist over here. Would you like to

buy one? She's only charging two dollars, which is a wise investment, if you ask me. You might even see her one day on Miss Morgan Trunk's TV show *Wise Investments with Morgan Trunk*. She's on channel nine."

How Littie learned to talk like that, I'll never know. But to my surprise, it works, because the man comes over to me and looks at my drawings. "What's this one supposed to be?" he asks, pointing to the egg.

I'm not sure if he doesn't know that it's an egg or not, or maybe he wants to know what kind of egg it is. So I say that it's an egg from a chicken. "A brown one."

He nods and scratches his chin. "Brown?"

"The egg, I mean, was brown," I say. "The chicken could be brown, too, but I never met her, so I'm not exactly sure."

He looks at the drawing with his head tilted to one side and then the other. Which doesn't make any sense to me, because any way you look at it, it's still an egg. Then he says, "Would you take a dollar?"

And I say, "Yes indeedy."

He hands me a crumpled-up dollar bill. I spread it out on my leg and smooth out the wrinkles. Then I fold it up again and slide it into my pocket.

"Only fourteen more of those and you'll have your necklace," Littie says.

I smile at Littie and tell her she should be president of the world someday. Then she says there is no such thing as president of the world and that it's important for the world to have many leaders, not just one. So I say, "Never mind, Littie. I was only trying to be nice."

"Oh," she says. "Thanks."

I'm not as good of a salesperson as Littie, I guess, because I'd rather watch cartoons than Morgan Trunk on TV. The only person I can get to look at my drawings is a lady who says she'll give me half of her burrito for the drawing of Terrible's sticker.

"You're not going to eat that, are you?" says

Littie, eyeballing the half burrito that I set on top of my toolbox. "You don't know where it's been."

"Not everything is dangerous, Littie."

"I know," she says. "But the other day when I was watching the news at your place, there was a report about nails in Halloween candy."

"It's not Halloween."

"Even so, I still wouldn't eat it. I'm just saying."

We sit cross-legged on the sidewalk and watch the sun slip behind the buildings across the street. A few people pass by, but the crowds are long gone, on their way to somewhere else. The sky glows orange and dims to gray, but nobody stops.

The man with the table of pocketbooks starts to pack up his things. "It's getting dark," I say to Littie.

"I should probably get home," she says. "Before Momma starts to worry."

"I'm going to have to tell Patsy Cline I don't have her necklace anymore." If there was any hope of being friends forever with Patsy, that hope is gone. There's no more holding on if there's nothing to hold on to. I pick up my drawings and am about to put them back inside my toolbox when somebody behind me says, "How much for that?"

I turn around. The man selling the pocketbooks waves at me and puts his sunglasses on the top of his red hat. Then he points to the burrito. "How much?"

"You want to buy the burrito?" I say.

"I would advise against it," says Littie. "It could have nails in it. I'm just saying."

"Not that, man," he says. "The box. How much for the box?"

"You want to buy my toolbox?" I say. "Oh, well, that's mine. I mean, it's not for sale."

"Twenty dollars," he says. "I'll give you twenty dollars for it."

I look at my toolbox, its rusty corners, chipped red paint.

Littie says, "Penelope, that's not for sale, is it?"

I never thought I could ever let go of my toolbox. It reminds me of my dad, and if I didn't have it, it might be like I didn't ever have him. And I might forget that he was ever here.

Grandpa Felix said sometimes you have to just let go.

But how do you know what to let go of? Letting go of Patsy Cline's necklace would mean letting go of Patsy Cline. I've already lost my dad, gone forever, and I can't lose her, too. I can't.

"What do you say?" says the man.

20.

No," I tell the man. "It's not for sale."

"Too bad." He shrugs and walks away like he can forget about the toolbox and won't be sitting up all night thinking about it and wishing he had it in bed next to him.

Littie puts her hand on my shoulder and says, "We'll find another way to get the money."

"How?"

Littie sighs and looks around. "I don't know exactly. But there has to be a way."

I nod and try to smile at her, but I don't see how

there is any other way. All I can see is Patsy Cline's face when I tell her that I broke her necklace. And then will she walk away from me, just like this man is walking away from my toolbox, to never think about me again?

I pick up my toolbox and press my fingers against the metal sides. I close my eyes, and in the dark I can see every rusty bump and blotch of chipped red paint. I can see how the paint has worn off where the handle rests against the lid. I can hear the click of the latch and the squeak of the handle when it swings.

"Come on," says Littie. "Let's go. Momma's going to be worried if I don't get home soon."

I follow Littie to the top of the escalators at the metro station. The steps churn down and keep churning. They don't stop. People push by me and are carried away by the stairs until I can only see the tops of their heads, and then they disappear altogether. Once I get on, there's no getting off. Littie grabs hold of the rail and is about to step onto the stair, but I grab her arm and pull her back. "Wait."

"What's the matter?" she says.

I undo the latch of my toolbox and hand Littie everything that's inside. "Hold this stuff for a second." Then I pull at the corners of the tape that's holding down the picture of my dad inside the lid. Real slowly, I peel off the picture, careful so it won't rip, and then fold back the tape around the edges of the picture. I tell my dad that I'm sorry, and then I slip him into my pocket.

"What are you doing?" says Littie.

But I can't look at her face, because if I do, I'll lose my nerve. "Go on home," I tell her. "Take my stuff with you, okay? I'm going back to the museum to get the necklace."

"You're going to do what?" she says.

Then I hug the toolbox to my chest and run at the man. His tables are gone, everything packed up, and he's closing the door to his van. "Wait!" I yell. "Don't go!"

"You change your mind about a bag?" he says.

I shake my head and hold my toolbox out to him. "Do you still want to buy this?"

"You'll let it go now, huh?"

I nod at him.

The man reaches into his pocket and pulls out a thick stack of dollars all rolled up. He unrolls it, pulls one from the stack and stuffs it into my hand. Then he reaches for my toolbox.

I think I hear Littie say my name when my fingers loosen their grip.

I let go. And as soon as I do, my dad is dead all over again. And then the tears come.

21.

I run all the way back to the museum. The air is colder now, and it stings my wet face. People look at me as I run by them, the kind of look that says, What's Wrong With That Poor Girl? Which makes me cry even harder.

Without my toolbox, I should be able to run faster, but my brains are full of concrete. Even my fingers know that something's missing. They curl around an invisible handle, pretending that everything is the same as always.

Grandpa Felix was wrong. You should never

let go. Because letting go means gone forever and you'll never get it back. I force my legs to keep going by thinking hard about Patsy Cline's necklace. And as my feet hit the sidewalk, I try to push away everything else in my brains—my toolbox, my dad, Grandpa Felix, and Alfred. Even Lumberjack Jack and how I'm going to get around him.

I race up the steps to the museum, grab the door handle with both hands, and pull. The door doesn't open. I run around to the side and try that door, but it's locked, too. The windows are dark, and I can't see anybody inside. I run back around to the front and beat my fists against the door. "Hello! Hello! Is anybody in there?" I shout loud enough even for Mangy Teddy to hear.

But no one comes.

22.

When I get to our apartment building, Littie is sitting at the top of the stairs waiting for me. The stuff from my toolbox is in a neat pile beside her. "Did you get it?" she whispers.

I shake my head. "I was too late."

Littie bites at her thumbnail. "Your mom just came over looking for you, and she looked really mad."

"Okay."

I pick up my things, everything that used to live in my toolbox but now has no place at all to live.

Littie walks me to the door to our apartment. "I'm sorry about your toolbox," she says.

"Me too."

Before I open our door, Littie says, "Wait!" She takes off the alarm from around her neck and puts it in my hand. "For your museum. But somehow I don't think you'll need it to remember me. I'm just saying."

I smile at her. "I don't think so either, Littie."

"It's just a loan, though. I'll need it back for our next adventure." And then she skips down the hall and slips into her apartment.

I take a deep breath and open our door. I can barely get a foot inside when I hear Terrible's voice say, "Mom, she's here!"

Mom's footsteps pound the hallway toward me, and before I can even take my coat off, Mom and Terrible are in front of me. "We need to talk," she says in a tone that I know means trouble.

Terrible has a grin on his face that says, Sit Back and Enjoy the Show. And I have a feeling that I'm the show.

"First of all, where have you been?" Mom says. "Did I not specifically say that your brother was in charge?"

"Yeah, I'm in charge," says Terrible, jabbing his thumb into his chest.

"You can't just leave whenever you want and go wherever you want without asking or at least telling someone, missy."

Good gravy. I'm missy again.

"Yeah. You're supposed to tell me," says Terrible, jabbing his chest again. "Because I'm in charge." Then he must have jabbed too hard, because he winces a little and rubs his chest.

Mom sighs. "Terrence?"

"Yeah, Mom?"

"Enough." She looks at me. "And second of all, and this is a big one, you can't take things from other people, things that don't belong to you. You're nine years old, almost ten, and you should know that by now."

"You're lucky you're not in jail," says Terrible. "For stealing." He puts his wrists together like he's been handcuffed and limps around in a circle.

Mom says, "Terrence?"

He stops limping. "Sorry."

"Stealing?" I say. "I didn't steal anything. Why does everybody think I'm stealing?"

"Who else thinks that?" says Mom.

"Lumberjack Jack. From the museum."

"You took something from the museum?" says Mom with a look that says, I'm Really Worried.

Terrible says, "We know what you did. I found your closet, dork."

My word.

"Terrence," says Mom, "why don't you call Grandpa Felix and tell him we found his camera and that she's okay."

"Okay," he says. Then he leans in close to me, so close that his smelly cologne makes me cough. "But if you ever go into my room again, I'll give you a reason to talk about dead things all the time."

"We'll see what NASA has to say about that."

And then I give him a look that says, That's Right, I Said NASA.

He rolls his eyeballs at me and walks away, but I can tell that he's worried. If there's one thing I know about aliens, it's that they are afraid of NASA.

Mom tells me to come sit next to her on the couch. Terrible is on the phone in the next room with Grandpa Felix, saying, "It's here. We've got it." And then "Penelope took it."

"Is Grandpa mad?"

"Do you know that we called the police and accused those painters of taking it?" says Mom.

"Oh."

"Oh, yes," she says. "Do you know what that camera is worth?"

I nod. "It's Grandpa's favorite. The first one he ever bought. We named it Alfred."

"That's not what I mean," she says. "That's a very expensive camera. It's worth a lot of money."

"That's not why I wanted it for my museum. I wanted it so that Grandpa Felix could be remembered. He said that what's worth something to him won't be worth anything to anybody else after he's dead, and I wanted to show him that's not true."

"Penelope Rae." (Stomach ulcer.) "Can we stop with the dead talk, please?"

"Sorry."

"Grandpa Felix is who you need to say you're sorry to," she says. "He's very upset."

My stomach sinks. "He is?"

"Well, how would you feel if you lost something that was important to you?" she says. "What if . . . what if . . . I don't know . . . what if your toolbox was gone?"

And that's when I start to cry again. Mom hugs me and asks me what this is all about. But I can barely get out the words. Eventually my eyes run out of water, and I catch my breath and tell her about Patsy Cline's necklace and my drawings and how Dad's toolbox is gone forever, just like him.

For some reason, Mom cries, too. And I think maybe she hasn't forgotten about Dad after all.

23.

Someone is knocking. "Come on in, Littie," I say from the middle of the Heap.

Only, it's not Littie at all. Patsy Cline peeks in and says, "Howdy." And then she says, "Looks like a pig moved in, had a party, and forgot to tip the maid."

Patsy Cline sure has a way of putting things. I'm going to miss that about her.

"What are you doing with all of this?" she says.

I point to my closet. "It's going back in there."

She peers around the Heap and into my closet. And reads out loud what's written in ultramarine letters. "Penelope Crumb's Ultra Museum of

Forget-Me-Notters." Then she looks at me like she's waiting for me to explain.

I don't know how to explain my museum without talking about her necklace, and I very much don't want to talk about her necklace. So I change the subject. "When's your next singing competition? Do you want to try on some of my shoes? Is it raining outside? Want to see my teeth collection?"

Patsy says, "My mom's waiting in the car, so I can't stay. We're on our way home from voice lessons, and I thought I could stop by and get my necklace. So I don't have to wait until Monday."

All of a sudden, I don't feel so good.

"You don't look so good," says Patsy. "Have you got the stomach bug?" She puts her hand over her mouth.

"I don't think so," I say, and then I remember how Patsy feels about germs (some of them have tails). "Actually, maybe I do." I pretend gag at her. "Maybe you should go—so you don't catch it, I mean."

Patsy holds her breath and puffs out her cheeks. Then she puts her hand out to me like she wants me to give up the necklace, but I pretend like I don't know what she wants.

Still holding her breath, Patsy waves her hand back and forth at me.

"Oh," I say, gagging again. And then I pretend to think that she wants to high-five, so I slap her hand.

She lets out her breath. "Ow!" Then she shakes the germs off her hand so they drip to the floor. "No, Penelope. My necklace." She looks around my room.

Good gravy. I push the closet door shut, but it gets caught on a pair of sandals.

Patsy pulls the neck of her shirt up over her mouth and then moves past me toward my closet. Under her shirt, she says something. It's muffled, but it sounds like, "What's a forget-me-notter, anyway?"

I try to block her, throw hang-up clothes in front of her, shake pretend germs on her, but there's not much that can sidetrack Patsy Cline when she's got her brains on something. She gets past me and sticks her head in my closet.

"Popsicle sticks!" she yells. "What is this place?" And then she finds the cards about her hair and necklace and she reads them out loud. With lots of exclamation points. Somehow having her in my museum, reading about her own things, makes me want to bury my head in the Heap and forget everything.

And then Patsy yells, "Yeeeeeaaaak!" Which is when I know she's found what's left of her necklace.

"I'm real sorry, Patsy," I say. "Real, real sorry."

She holds the chain in one hand and the pile of sand in the other. "What in blazes happened to it?"

"Littie found my museum and saw that I had your necklace, and I told her I was going to give it back to you and then I was taking it from her, and I hardly touched it, but sand dollars break really easy, and that's what happened."

Patsy shakes her head. "But something doesn't figure. Why would you put my necklace in your museum if you were going to give it back to me? And what kind of museum only has a necklace and a hair in it?" She picks up the heart-shaped tin. "And teeth?"

"Oh, no. Your necklace was one of the first things I got. The teeth were just for protection and in case your necklace got a case of the lonelies," I say. "I had other stuff in there, too. A sketchbook from my mom, drawings from Terrible, an Alfred camera from my grandpa Felix, and a shoehorn from my dad. But I had to give them all back. Well, except for the shoehorn."

"Wait a second," Patsy says. "But I thought you just found my necklace yesterday."

I close my eyes and tell the truth. "I might have found it a couple of days ago."

Patsy sucks in a bunch of air and it makes a high-pitched screech. But no words come out.

So I fill up the empty space with how sorry I am and that I should have told her sooner that I found it, but truth be told, I wanted to keep the necklace, not for me, but to remember her by because Vera Bogg was taking her away. Then I reach into my pocket and hand her the twenty dollars I got for my toolbox. "Here," I say. "I was going to buy you a new necklace with this, but the museum was closed."

Patsy takes the money without even saying thank you. Then she stuffs the silver chain, the sand, and the money into her back pocket. She steps over the clothes from the Heap and heads for the door.

"Wait," I say, my arms reaching. "Please."

And to my surprise, she turns around. For a second, I think she is going to hug me and promise me she'll be back over tomorrow and we can have a staring contest, which she will definitely win. And things will be back to the way they were.

But there are no hugs or promises. Instead, she goes back inside my closet and takes her hair, the last proof that she was my best friend. On her way out of my room, Patsy gives me a look that says, I Won't Forget About This.

I really hope that she does.

24.

The next morning, just after the sun comes up, Mom drives me to Grandpa Felix's apartment. I cup Alfred in my hands and tell him he'll be home soon.

Mom is quiet for most of the way, until we're almost to Grandpa's, when she says, "It's not easy being you, is it?"

I shrug. "I don't know how to be anybody else."

She nods and gives me half of a smile. "I guess that's true."

"I think Patsy Cline thinks I'm weird," I say.

"Why do you say that?"

I look at the people on the sidewalk, passing by our car window. People I don't know and who don't know me. "Because I'm not Vera Bogg."

Mom says that she doesn't know what that means or what a Vera Bogg is. I tell her that Vera Bogg isn't a what, she's a who. And Mom says, "The only who you need to worry about being is Penelope Crumb. And that should be good enough for anybody."

But I don't think that's good enough for Patsy Cline.

Mom says, "You made some changes to my sketches. You didn't think they were good enough?"

"They are good," I tell her. "But your eyes were closed. I wanted to remember your eyes."

Mom shakes her head and gives me a look that says, I Don't Know What I'm Going to Do With You.

"What's it like being you?" I ask.

She squints her eyes like she's really giving her

brains a workout and takes a while to come up with an answer. When she pulls up to the curb outside of Grandpa's apartment, she says, "Challenging. Some of the time." Then she strokes my hair. "But also pretty wonderful."

"Maybe it's not easy being anybody. Even dead people have the problem of being forgotten," I say. "And also the problem of being dead."

For a second, I think Mom is going to say a word I'm not supposed to hear because there I go again talking about dead things. But instead she just laughs a little and says, "You know what, Penelope? You're probably right."

I push open the car door. It's not going to be easy with Grandpa Felix, that's for sure.

"Are you sure you don't want me to come in with you?" Mom says.

I grip Alfred with both hands and shake my head. "I think I'll be okay."

She says, "I think so, too."

I hug Alfred to my chest with one hand and

knock on Grandpa's door with the other. It takes four more knocks until I can hear his footsteps. Which means he's been sleeping his life away again.

He opens the door, and I try to look him right in the eye, the way he's always telling me to do. But it's hard when you've done wrong. Grandpa Felix looks at me and then at Alfred.

He holds out his hand and I put Alfred in it. "You've got something to say, then?" he says.

I tell him I'm sorry for taking Alfred, awful sorry, and for getting his painters in trouble with the police.

"Were you aiming to sell it or something?" The lines in his face are deep, like made by a river a long time ago before it dried up and disappeared. "I didn't think you of all people would ever do something like that, Penelope."

I just about go dead right then and there. I try to explain about my museum, about holding on, but it doesn't really matter, I guess, because in the end, I took something that didn't belong to me.

"You can't hold on to things that belong to

someone else," he says. "In some way or another, they always end up finding their way back to their owner."

"Is that so?" I say. Because then maybe someday my toolbox will come back to me.

"I don't know. It sounds good, doesn't it?" He tells me to come inside and take a load off. Now that I don't have my toolbox anymore, I don't have a load to take off, but I go in anyway.

At first I think I'm in the wrong place. "What happened?" I say. "Your piles are gone!"

Grandpa Felix says, "Coffee?" And then when I say no, he says, "Smart girl."

"Grandpa, where did everything go?"

He takes a sip from his mug. "I'll tell you something. You might have done me a favor by taking Alfred, in a way. I tore up this place looking for it, and while I was doing that, I got to looking at all of my pictures. And I decided it was time to do something with them." He goes over to his bookshelf and pulls out a stack of books. He brings them over to the table and opens the one on top.

"You put them in albums," I say, turning the pages.

He says, "Now they have a proper place to live."

"Forever." The pictures are three to a page, and some I don't remember seeing before. Most are of people I don't know, or birds, or lizards, or flowers so close up, you can almost smell them.

There's one picture that stands out from the others, and not because it's prettier or anything like that. But because it's different. This picture is of a tree. One that is brown, all the leaves gone. Its empty branches needle the sky as if to say, Doesn't Anybody Care About Me?

"What's this dead tree for?" I ask.

Grandpa leans in close and looks at the picture. He chews on his lip for a while, and finally when one of his brain wrinkles finds the answer, he says, "That tree isn't dead, Penelope. Why do you always think everything is dead?"

"I don't know," I say. "Sometimes they just are."

"This tree is in a winter slumber."

"Slumber?"

"It's asleep," he explains.

"Oh."

He stares at the picture for a long time. "This was the tree in our backyard. I grew up with it. Used to climb to the top to hide from everyone. I'd spend hours up there reading comic books and taking pictures. It's a strange thing to miss a tree."

"But now you can look at it anytime you want," I say.

He smiles, and the lines in his face aren't so deep. "And I can remember."

"Mayor Luckett's eyeglasses!" I say, smacking my hand down on the album.

"What?"

"This! Your pictures!" I say.

"What about them?"

"They are just like Maynard C. Portwaller's gray hair, and just like Mangy Teddy, and even the wedding pictures you take. They help you always remember, so you never forget."

"Maybe so," he says, rubbing the whiskers on his chin.

"It's like your very own museum!" I say. Right then, I wish I had a picture of my toolbox. I tell Grandpa Felix this, but just when he says, "What happened to your toolbox?" I say, "Quick! Can I have a piece of paper and a pencil?"

While Grandpa looks for them, I close my eyes and picture my toolbox, its creaky handle and rusty corners. He takes forever to find some. I can hear him shuffling around the room and saying, "Paper. Hmmm. Paper. Envelopes? Nope. Paper. Hmmm. Paper. Where would I have some paper?" After a long time, he says, "There you are." And I open my eyes.

I take the picture of my toolbox that I have in my brain and draw it on the paper, remembering all the chipped red paint parts. It may not be the same as having the toolbox in my hands, but at least now I know I won't forget about it.

Mister Leonardo da Vinci would surely approve.

I show the picture to Grandpa Felix and explain about selling my dad's toolbox. Before the toolbox was my dad's, though, it belonged to Grandpa Felix, and I worry that he's going to miss it as much as me. But all he says is "humph" and nothing else. Then he gets up from the table, pulls another album from his bookshelf, and drops it in my lap.

I turn to the first page, but it's blank. No pictures.

"For you," he says, tapping the album with his knuckles. "Your own museum."

I throw my arms around his neck. His whiskers scrape my cheek. I whisper in his ear, "Thank you, Grandpa."

He pats me on the back and clears his throat. "Now you can go ahead and put your toolbox drawing in there. And anything else you want to remember, I guess."

I reach into my pocket and pull out the picture of my dad that was taped inside my toolbox. I slide it into the album and say, "Here's a nice new home for you, Daddy."

My brain wrinkles are busy thinking about what pictures and drawings I can put in my new museum. So I'll always remember and never forget. And one brain wrinkle must shout out, "Patsy Cline," because right away I think of her and how she took herself out of my museum.

And then I get another piece of paper from Grandpa and start a new drawing. So I can put her back.

Why Museums Are Important to Me
By Penelope Crumb

Museums are important to me because they help you remember about people, places, and things that happened. And they are full of wonder. The Portwaller History Museum made me wonder about the people who used to live in our town and what they were like, what toys they played with, and that the first mayor had a tiny nose but a really big body. And also he wore glasses. Which were right there in the museum for everybody to see. (Which is okay if the family says it's allowed.)

Some museums are full of things that belonged to dead people. But other museums are full of things from people who aren't dead yet (but will be one day) but who should be remembered because they are great.

I know lots of people who should be

remembered even though their stuff isn't in any museum. But I don't think a museum has to be a building or even a closet. It can be anything, like a photo album even. Because drawings and pictures can help you remember. And that way you'll never forget.

The End

Turn the page for a peek at the next book
featuring PENELOPE CRUMB!

1.

Sometimes I worry about getting the Bad Luck. I don't know how you catch the Bad Luck exactly, but I guess it's a lot like catching the stomach flu. Or getting warts. (Truth be told, if you've got the stomach flu AND warts, then your luck probably isn't so good.)

Some people seem to have the Bad Luck an awful lot of the time. Except for my dad being Graveyard Dead and me having an alien for a brother, my luck has been pretty okay up until now. Not real good, but not real bad either. That's the way I like it. Because here's one thing I know about the Bad Luck:

It comes right along with the Good Luck. You can't have one without the other.

Which makes me nervous, because today has a lot of the Good Luck in it:

1. *Mom left for work early.*
2. *Orange Popsicle for breakfast. For real, two.*
3. *Found long-lost T-shirt in rag bag. Still fits except for part that covers my stomach.*
4. *Alien overslept and missed bus.*
5. *Two orange Popsicles in lunchbox. For real, four.*
6. *No surprise test on decimal points.*
7. *Angus Meeker home sick with the stomach flu.*
8. *Not one mean comment about how big my nose is.*
9. *Patsy Cline smiled at me.*

With all that good stuff, I just know that the Bad Luck is right around the corner. But I can't think about corners so much right now because Miss Stunkel is letting us use clay in art class. And so I am busy making a cow.

Patsy Cline Roberta Watson, my used-to-be best

friend, is crazy about cows. Instead of spots like real cows have, I draw hearts in the clay with my pencil point. Just because.

I set the cow on the corner of my desk, so it's as close to Patsy Cline as it can be without jumping over the space between our desks. Patsy Cline is smushing her clay into something that could be a worm that's been run over by a delivery truck. Or else a horse with pneumonia. Patsy Cline isn't so good at art.

I make a *cuuullllggggh* noise with my throat and wait for Patsy to look this way. She does, thank lucky stars, but she has a look on her face that says, You Should Cover Your Mouth.

"Sorry," I say, even though I am really not sorry because it was only a pretend cough and therefore only pretend germs that Patsy doesn't need to be afraid of. "But look." I point to the cow.

When she sees it, her eyes get big and almost weepy and she says, "Oh, how I wish cows had hearts like that in real life."

Which makes me smile.

But then Vera Bogg, who is Patsy Cline's brand-new best friend, crinkles up her teeny nose and says, "But cows *do* have hearts, Patsy Cline."

Good gravy. That's Vera Bogg for you.

With her pink fingernail, Vera presses a smiley face into a small ball and then stacks it on top of two others. "I think it would be better if you made it more like a real-looking cow," Vera says to me, pushing her pink headband back on her head. "And where's its tail?"

I am about to tell Vera a thing or two about art, about Patsy Cline, and about cows, but instead I flatten the cow with my fist. If Vera Bogg doesn't know that art doesn't have to be real-looking, that everybody knows cows have hearts *on the inside,* and that Patsy Cline is allergic to things with tails, then I'm not going to be the one to tell her.

Miss Stunkel walks up and down the rows, and when she gets to my desk, she looks at my flattened cow and says, "Penelope, you've made a pancake? How *nice.*" Only, she says it in a way that makes me think she only eats waffles.

She nods at Patsy Cline's sick horse as she passes, which is now just about dead, and then stops right in front of Vera Bogg. "Oh, Vera," she says. "What a delightful snowman. You're really something." And she makes a big deal out of the *something*.

Vera Bogg's face gets as pink as the rest of her. It's the kind of pink that makes me feel like a raw hot dog. The sort that makes you sick if you don't cook it long enough. Vera Bogg is Miss Stunkel's All-Time Favorite. She'd have to be to get a big-deal *something* for a boring old snowman.

If Mister Leonardo da Vinci was here, he would surely say, "It seems apparent to me, oh me oh my, that Miss Stunkel couldn't tell a craggy rock from a masterpiece." Because that's how dead artists talk.

Then Vera Bogg starts telling Patsy Cline how wonderful Patsy's clay sculpture is, and how she wishes she could make something that good. I can't help but roll my eyeballs. Even Patsy Cline looks a little suspicious, but then she says, "Do you know what it's supposed to be?"

Vera's eyes get wide, and after staring at the lump

on Patsy's desk for a long time, she says, "Well, it looks like it could be a lot of things."

"It's a fiddle," says Patsy Cline.

"That's just what I was going to say," says Vera. "A fiddle."

Patsy Cline nods and smiles, and all I can do is shake my head. Because how Vera Bogg, and not me, can be Patsy's All-Time Favorite is something I will never ever understand.

Meanwhile, I'm molding my pancake into a hungry tiger, which I plan on training to bite at Vera Bogg's ankles, and Miss Stunkel says she has an important announcement so listen up.

A man with a beard that's just on his chin and not on his cheeks comes into the classroom and sits on top of Miss Stunkel's desk. Not in a chair, but on her desk. Which I don't think Miss Stunkel likes too well because she gives him a look that says, Chairs Are Chairs for a Reason.

Miss Stunkel says, "I'd like to introduce you all to Mr. Rodriguez. He is visiting schools in our area to talk about an exciting new art project."

Right away my ears perk up.

Mr. Rodriguez swings his legs and smiles. "Hey," he says. "So, like Miss Stinkel said . . ."

"Stunkel," says Miss Stunkel, and she points her chicken-bone finger at us to make sure none of us thinks that's funny. Even though it very much is the funniest thing ever.

"Sorry, wrong tense," says Mr. Rodriguez, clearing his throat. "Stunkel. Anyway, I'm going all around town to get some volunteers to help with an art project. We're painting a mural at Portwaller's Blessed Home for the Aging."

"Ooh." I drop the tiger and raise my hand high.

Mr. Rodriguez smiles at me, and then Miss Stunkel tells me to hold on and that Mr. Rodriguez is not finished. But I don't need to hear anything else, because I would paint a mural on the moon. On a moon rock. On a MoonPie, even. I, Penelope Crumb, am going to be a famous artist when I grow up, and painting murals is what famous artists do. Just ask Leonardo da Vinci. (Which you could do if he wasn't already dead.)

"The theme of the mural is Mother Goose," says Mr. Rodriguez, "and if you want to do this, you have to show up for the next couple Saturdays and Sundays. So, if you have soccer practice or lunch with Grandma every Sunday, you'll probably have to make other plans." He swings his legs again and smiles. Then he says how it will mean so much to all of the people in the Blessed Home for the Aging and how they don't have so much to live for anymore, seeing how they are so old and almost dead.

Miss Stunkel rubs her Thursday lizard pin and says, "So, if this sounds like something you'd like to participate in, raise your hand."

My hand is still up, but Miss Stunkel is busy looking around the room and writing down the names of other kids on a piece of paper. I stick my other hand in the air and make big circles so she won't miss me. And it works, too, because Mr. Rodriguez points right at me and says to Miss Stunkel, "There's a live one over there."

Miss Stunkel sighs and says, "Penelope Crumb, I've already got your name on the list. So unless you're trying to message Mars, please put your hands down."

Everybody laughs, which makes my cheeks burn. But then Mr. Rodriguez scratches his chin beard and says to me, "I think it's pretty righteous that you're so excited about art."

Righteous. I don't know what that means exactly, but it sounds like he thinks I'm right. Which is something Miss Stunkel never says I am. I smile and give him a look that says, Please Tell My Teacher That She Is Very Wrongeous. And it's a good thing that Miss Stunkel isn't very good at telling what different kinds of faces mean because I would definitely get a note sent home for that one.

That's when Patsy Cline raises her hand and says, "What if you aren't any good at drawing?"

Which really is a surprise. Not because Patsy Cline isn't any good at drawing—she's not—but that she would even want to do an art project at all. Especially on Saturdays and Sundays when her mom makes her practice for singing competitions.

Mr. Rodriguez says, "That's nothing to worry about. And I bet you're better than you think."

She isn't.

Patsy Cline smiles and gives me a look that says, Maybe I'm Not So Bad After All. I put on a smile that says, Well, You're Definitely Not the Worst, Patsy Cline. Because that's the truth. And even if it wasn't, that's the kind of thing you say to your used-to-be best friend. Especially when you'd like more than anything to get her back.

And then I think what good luck this is because now I'll have Patsy Cline all to myself, thank lucky stars. And after she sees me paint, she will surely say, "Penelope Crumb, you are my Favorite, because you are the most wonderful artist, and I was so wrong to throw you over for Vera Bogg, because anybody who wears that much pink can't be right in the head."

But then the Bad Luck peeks out at me from around the corner. Because the next thing I see is Vera Bogg raising her hand.

Maybe it's those pink fingernails, but all I can think of is that I don't want the Bad Luck to get any closer. And the next thing I know, the tiger is in my hand, but only for a second because then it leaps at Vera.

And I have to say, for an untrained tiger, it's pretty good. The tiger knocks her hand down and then hits her desk and falls to the floor. I think its head falls off, poor thing. And Vera screams.

That's when I know the Bad Luck has found me for certain, because Miss Stunkel pulls out her chicken-bone finger and points it at me and says I can be sure she's sending a note home.

And in case you missed it,
be sure to pick up the first book in the
PENELOPE CRUMB series!

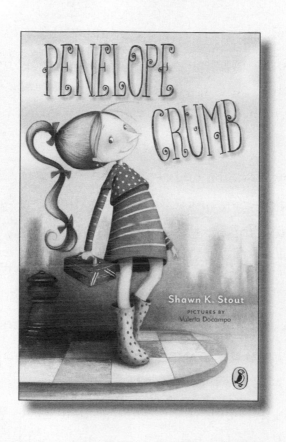

acknowledgments

I have a good memory.

I can remember all kinds of things from when I was a kid. Like how I used to gnaw on a stick of butter at the dinner table. And how I caught my finger in a door during a camping trip when I was seven and my whole fingernail fell off. And chopping down the tree in our front yard during a blizzard. And changing my shoes and cardigan sweater when I got home from school so that Mister Rogers would one day let me live in his neighborhood. And making a basket for my mom for Mother's

Day, where I glued on a picture of myself, as well as some of my hair and a bloody tooth from my collection. (She still has this basket.) And how my sister took me to the mall to jump in one of those inflatable moon bounce things, and then left me there.

My sister says I make things up.

I think probably we're both right. But what I will never forget are the people who have loved and supported me, and provided inspiration (and much-needed childcare) during the writing of this book. In particular, my mom, Heidi Potterfield, Jerry and Shirley Stout, MaryAnn Mundey, Carol Dowling, Lori Thibault, Amy Cabrera, and Charlotte Hartley. Thanks also to my writerly friends and second family at Vermont College of Fine Arts, especially Jess Leader, Annemarie O'Brien, Micol Ostow, Gene Brenek, Mary Quattlebaum, Tami Lewis Brown, Sarah Aronson, Leda Schubert, Tim Wynne-Jones, Rita Williams-Garcia, Uma Krishnaswami, and Kathi Appelt. Special thanks to Erin Loomis, who makes me laugh until I cry and is the only other person I know who shares my deep-rooted affection for fried bologna sandwiches, John Denver, and spygear.

I owe a great deal of thanks to Andy, for his love, partnership, encouragement, and his ability to answer questions like, "What's a museum called that only has things in it that are important to one person? Is that a real thing?"

Much thanks to my wonderful editor, Jill Santopolo, and to everyone at Philomel, who have made this such an amazing experience. And to my lovely agent, Sarah Davies at Greenhouse Literary Agency, thank you for believing in me.